E.J. RUSSELL

# FIVE DEAD HERRINGS

QUEST INVESTIGATIONS
BOOK ONE

Five Dead Herrings
Copyright © 2021 by E.J. Russell

Cover art: L.C. Chase, http://lcchase.com
Edited by Meg DesCamp

ISBN: 978-1-947033-33-7

First edition
September, 2021

Contact information:
ejr@ejrussell.com

E.J. RUSSELL

# FIVE DEAD HERRINGS

QUEST INVESTIGATIONS
BOOK ONE

*Dedicated to my readers who thought Matt deserved his own story, and to Dorothy L. Sayers, for title inspiration I couldn't resist.*

# CHAPTER
## ONE

I've been parked behind a scraggly thimbleberry bush for the last six hours with my camera pointed at a tree.

And when I say "parked," I'm not talking about the marginal comfort of my beater Honda. No, I'm talking about my butt planted on a clump of grass that looked soft(ish) when I showed up for this stakeout at dawn, but that now feels more like a pile of rocks.

You having a hard time putting that information together? I mean, *camera* plus *stakeout* might give you the idea that I'm a private investigator, right? Or a paparazzo. Or maybe a peeping tom. And you'd be sorta right for two out of three (okay, maybe three out of three, but I wasn't *intentionally* peeping), depending on where in my personal timeline you landed.

Because I wasn't a paparazzo, per se. I didn't stalk celebutantes or pop stars or actors with personal restraint issues. No fewer than three tabloids had me on their starred contributor list because I was Matt Steinitz, the most successful cryptid photographer in the world. Okay, in America. Well…in the Pacific Northwest.

*Fine.* In Oregon, okay? West of the Cascades, anyway.

But it wasn't my modest success in cryptid photography that got me my current gig with Quest Investigations. No, it was being mistaken for a guy who was a *real* success—not to mention a real douchebag—and the only thing that saved me from some kind of arcane punishment was the fact his photographs were crap.

Did you catch that part about Quest Investigations? So, yeah, I'm *working* for private investigators, but I'm not an investigator myself. I'm their surveillance guy. Which makes me...a professional peeping tom.

It'd be sleazy if it wasn't so goddamn *boring*.

Like now. Because I was staking out a *tree*. And not even an *interesting* tree. I mean, a pink flowering dogwood in the spring? I could happily stare at one of those all day long. A Doug fir in winter, with the wind tossing its branches and maybe a little snow spangling its needles? Sign me up. But my target today— in mid-September, when everything is tired, hot, and dusty— was a specimen of *Ailanthus altissima*, aka the *tree of heaven*, and that was about as big an oxymoron as jumbo shrimp or business intelligence.

Yet here I was, on the one hand wishing my coffee thermos wasn't empty and on the other hand—or maybe the same one— wishing I hadn't drunk all of it because now I needed to offload some of that, if you catch my drift, and I didn't want to, well, piss where I sat. But if I ducked behind the nearest *interesting* tree for a little relief, who'd keep the camera pointed at the lousy tree of heaven?

"Next time," I muttered as I shifted uncomfortably, "I'm bringing a tripod."

You'd be forgiven for asking why I'm putting myself through this, other than, you know, a paycheck, which is a completely fair question. Here's the deal.

Apparently some dryad outraged her clan by cheating. And we're not talking about a clandestine hookup at a cheap motel near the airport, or even a high class liaison at an upscale B&B out on the coast. Nope. According to her clan chief—a guy who, since he's a dryad, probably has a *literal* stick up his ass—she's allegedly cheating on her *tree*.

Did you know anyone could cheat on a tree? Yeah, me neither. Especially since dryads aren't exactly...is there a word for cleaving solely to one particular tree? Treemogamous? Arboreallegiant? Dryads can merge with any tree whose trunk circumference is bigger than their waist, but Stick-Up-His-Ass was in a major state about this one: "It's an *invasive species!*"

To tell you the truth, I expected my bosses to turn the case down. You might have heard of these two guys—Niall O'Tierney and Mal Kendrick. That's *Prince* Niall and *Lord* Maldwyn, because Niall's brother is the freaking King of Faerie, and Mal's a high-up fae too—he was the Queen's Enforcer for two hundred years.

So this is my life now. I work for fae royalty.

Not only that but Zeke Oz, our office manager? Demon. Yep, you heard that right, although the only scary thing about him is his efficiency. He's the sweetest guy you'd ever want to meet.

Well, okay, not *the* sweetest. That would be the grizzly shifter I was crushing on for years before he got married.

I know what you're thinking and stop, okay? Just stop.

Because you're right. I'm still crushing on him. I know nothing'll ever come of it. But if you knew Ted, you'd be in love with him too. I don't know how everybody on the *planet* isn't in love with him. His incubus husband is one lucky devil.

Did you catch that? Incubus. Husband.

That's right. They're all real. Dryads. Shifters. Fae. Incubi. Demons. Angels—although I don't recommend them; the only one I've met was a total douchecanoe. Druids. *Vampires*, for Pete's sake.

And me, you ask? Garden variety, dirt common, 100% ordinary human.

I should count myself lucky, right? I dreamed of this stuff from the time I was a kid. That's why I spent so much time tracking down cryptid sightings when I still worked for the tabloids. I just wanted it to be *real*, you know? Now that I've discovered it is, and that I'm literally the only human allowed to regularly interact with the wider supernatural community— supes, they call themselves—I should be happy.

And I am. Mostly. I'm amazed daily at how *cool* it all is, but at the same time, I'm reminded that I'll never be anything more than an outsider. An observer. Quest Investigations' pet human.

In fact, when I told you I *was* Matt Steinitz—past tense? According to my passport and driver's license and credit card bills, I still am. But at Quest, everybody knows me as Hugh. Hugh Mann.

It began as a slur. When I first started with Quest, clients would often look down their noses at me and say, *"What is that* human *doing here?"* Mal, who can never resist a joke, started calling me Hugh. I thought it was his way of—as he'd put it— taking the mickey out of them. But Zeke told me it was also to protect me: Supes have very long memories and some of them might resent me if they found out about my tabloid work. Mal didn't want me to be a target.

To be honest, I kind of like the extra name. For one thing, it keeps me honest: I'm not one of them, and I never will be. For another, it means that Ted—my grizzly shifter crush—is the only one who still calls me Matt. Pathetic, I know. But it means he *sees* me, at least a little, and since that's all I can ever expect from him, I'll take whatever crumbs I can catch.

I sighed, shifting to my right butt cheek to give the left one a break. I still wasn't sure why Quest took this job. Maybe it was because Stick-Up-His-Ass was bugging Mal's husband, who's not only a druid but also an environmental science professor. That seemed unlikely though, since Dr. MacLeod never had trouble telling people to piss right off if he thought they were being jerks.

I had a sneaking suspicion this whole case was nothing but busy work. They took it to give me something to do because they got tired of me moping around the office.

"Hey, Hugh!"

I nearly fell over sideways at the cheerful greeting, fumbling my camera and barely saving it from falling onto a rock.

"Jordan?" I stared up at the fresh-faced kid in the Wonderful Mug coffee shop T-shirt. He had a takeout bag from the Mediterranean restaurant next to the Quest offices in his hand. "What are you doing here? And for god's sake, get *down!*"

The young werewolf—yeah, *werewolf*—immediately hunkered down next to me, the bag crinkling loudly in the quiet woods. He gazed around, his brown eyes wide. "Sorry!" His whisper probably carried all the way to the coast. He held up the bag like a trophy. "I brought you lunch."

My stomach rumbled in response to the delicious aroma of perfectly cooked falafel. "Thanks, but why?" Usually Zeke handles our meals in the field. Jordan isn't a Quest employee. He's just a college kid—okay, college werewolf—who works part time at a coffee shop. "And for that matter, how?"

He rolled his eyes. "I got here the same as you. The FTA."

Niall's brother, the new King of Faerie, started a highly lucrative business for his subjects—the Fae Transportation Association. You can get pretty much anywhere that's not excessively public by taking a shortcut through Faerie. Jordan had it right—that's how I got here myself. But a lot of the FTA "drivers" were really, really big and obviously not human. In other words, not exactly unobtrusive.

"Jordan," I murmured, "you realize this is a *stakeout*, right? It won't do much good if the target figures out she's being watched, and hearing a trow or a duergar crashing around in the underbrush is a dead giveaway."

He frowned. "I'm not *stupid*, Hugh. I had him drop me off a ways away. Besides, I requested a subcompact ride."

I blink at him. "Subcompact?" What the heck? "You can't *request* a specific kind of driver on a random pickup."

He beamed at me. "You can now! Hector upgraded the FTA app."

I narrowed my eyes. "Does Dr. MacLeod know you're still using that app? Does he know Hector is still messing with the magic grid even after he was specifically told to lay off?"

Jordan bit his lip. "Not exactly."

Which meant not at all. Honestly, *kids*. Although I suppose they're not technically kids. Jordan was almost twenty-one, and his friend Hector—another werewolf—probably a year or so older. But young werewolves—juniors, they were called—had such a...*puppyish* way about them that it was hard to remember sometimes.

I was only thirty-six, but I always felt about ninety whenever I was around Jordan. Any minute now, I'd start growling at him to get off my lawn. Or maybe not. Because this patch of grass? He could have it with my blessing.

He handed me the bag. "I stopped by your office to pick up the pastry trays from that big meeting yesterday. Zeke was busy, so I offered to do the delivery." His brown eyes sparkled. "Your job must be so exciting. Who are we spying on?" He bounced a little on his haunches. "Oooh! Oooh! Is it Sasquatch?"

"Not this time." I smiled wryly. Ted used to imitate Sasquatch by partially shifting and lurking in the woods near his place. He was lonely back then and trying to attract someone to talk to. It certainly worked on me. He hooked me like a lovesick trout. "A tree."

Jordan's face fell. "A tree?"

"Yup." I pointed to the tree of my-own-personal-purgatory. "That one right there."

He wrinkled his nose. "Ugh. Those are so stinky."

"You can smell it?"

"Can't you?"

Ah. Right. Werewolves had a heightened sense of smell. "No." I shifted uncomfortably, my bladder reminding me of my earlier coffee intake. I eyed Jordan, who was frowning at the tree. Since he was here, I might as well take advantage of it. "Say, Jordan, can you do me a favor?"

Immediately, he brightened. "Sure! Just name it."

I handed him the camera. "Keep this focused on the tree and if the dryad emerges"—I pointed to the shutter release button —"press this and hold it."

"Wow." His expression was almost reverent as he took the camera. "I've never been an assistant spy before."

I buried a snort. Jordan was even less unobtrusive than trows and duergar. "I won't be a minute. Just gotta duck behind a bush for a bit, if you know what I mean."

He nodded sagely, but I'm not sure he really got it. "Sure thing, Hugh."

Nevertheless, I checked to make sure his fingers weren't blocking the lens before I crept away, keeping low and moving as silently as possible in the underbrush.

I took care of business, which lasted a little longer than I anticipated—hey, I drank *a lot* of coffee, okay?—and slunk back toward my stakeout blind, keeping my head down. But when I got to the thimbleberry, Jordan wasn't there. I would have thought that I'd mistaken the spot, except the falafel sack was there, as was my camera bag.

But not Jordan. And not my camera.

I peered through the screen of leaves. The tree of heaven looked just as boring and just as dryad-free as it had all day.

"Jordan," I muttered, "where the heck are you and where's my camera?"

I spotted a flash of white about thirty yards to my right, completely out of sight of the target, and controlled my urge to roll my eyes. "Seriously, Jordan?" I murmured. The white wasn't his Wonderful Mug T-shirt. No, that would be his bare chest. I couldn't see below his waist, thank goodness, but I expected his pants were gone too.

"Get back here!" I hissed, but he was either too far away to hear or he was deliberately ignoring me. He brandished the camera and then beckoned and pointed in some kind of weird and totally unintelligible sign language.

I held up my hands, palms up, in a helpless shrug. He scrunched up his face and then made an exaggerated point of setting my camera down carefully.

"Don't do it. Don't do it!" I muttered.

But we were talking about Jordan so of course he did it. He shifted, and suddenly there was a lean gray wolf with a white blaze on his flank slinking through the underbrush.

"Goddamnit." I took off in a low crouch toward my camera and reached it just as Jordan paused by the tree of heaven. And lifted his leg.

"Are you *kidding* me?"

But after a morning of no action whatsoever, I couldn't risk missing an opportunity. If I were a dryad and a werewolf peed on my shoes...roots...whatever, it would probably provoke a reaction. I raised my camera to catch the fallout.

But nothing happened.

Jordan cast a glance over his shoulder, and even though he was a wolf, that expression was nothing short of cheeky. He continued past the now-watered tree of heaven toward a massive Pacific madrone about a dozen yards further on. He sniffed around the base, then raised his head and caught my gaze, holding it long enough that I got the message.

I pointed the camera at the same time he lifted his leg and—

"Holy crap!"

A dryad burst out of the madrone, knocking Jordan head over tail. Jordan's yip and sharp whine almost made me miss the shot. But then another dryad charged out, and another, and another.

"It's like some freaking woodland clown car," I muttered as I rushed toward where Jordan had landed against the base of a maple.

By this time, there were about a dozen dryads dressed in Robin Hood grunge, milling around, shouting, and waving their arms like trees in a windstorm. Then they all spotted me and froze.

"Human," one of them choked out.

*Uh oh.*

"Jordan," I called, "run!"

He didn't hesitate, and neither did I. I looped my camera strap around my neck and high tailed it toward the spot where my FTA driver had dropped me off before dawn. Jordan was streaking along beside me, still in wolf form, and I noticed he was favoring one paw. But with a dozen really angry and freaked out dryads behind us, I couldn't take the time to check on him. Jordan's clothes, my camera bag, my abandoned lunch —all of those would have to wait until we'd shaken the posse off our tails.

See, there's this thing. It's called the Secrecy Pact. Humans aren't allowed to know about the supernatural community, and any supe who violates it is subject to Spanish Inquisition-level punishment. If the dryads caught me—if they caught Jordan—I doubted they'd wait long enough for me to pull out my Quest credentials, assuming they'd believe them, and assuming that didn't piss them off even more.

I shoved my hand in my jacket pocket—not an easy thing to do when running hell for leather—and pulled out an oak leaf with a Celtic rune embossed on it in gold. "Cl-cludo," I panted.

Nothing happened. *Crap.* I needed to stop and catch my breath enough to invoke the spell with the correct pronunciation. Magic was totally cool, but it was really, *really* specific, and stricter than my eighth grade math teacher.

Behind us, the dryads weren't just plowing haphazardly through the underbrush like Jordan and me. Their progress sounded more like the Columbus Day wind storm, and the trees around us were starting to lash too, even though there was no actual wind. I pulled to a stop in the middle of a clearing, although I was still way too close to the surrounding trees for my peace of mind. I felt a little like Dorothy about to get smacked by the apple tree, although I had an uneasy suspicion that these trees—Doug fir and red alder and western hemlock—wouldn't stop at a mere hand slap.

In fact, one massive branch swung at us. "Get back!" I twisted, pushing Jordan behind me. The branch whooshed past, barely missing me—although it didn't miss my camera. I heard the crack and winced, but with a gang—herd? grove?—of warlike dryads bearing down on us, I didn't have time to assess the damage.

"Cludo!" I shouted, and began to count *one one thousand*. The first dryad burst into the clearing. *Two one thousand*. She bared her extremely pointed teeth as her fingers sprouted bark and thorns like blackberry brambles. *Three one thou—*

"Where to?" A massive trow appeared between me and the ravening dryads.

"Quest Investigations. Fourth floor. And hurry." I grabbed Jordan's ruff.

The driver glanced at the approaching dryads. "Them too? That'll cost extra."

"No! Just me and the were. *Now* please!"

He shrugged. "It's your gold." He gestured with one massive hand, and when the portal opened, Jordan and I tumbled through into Faerie.

# CHAPTER TWO

An hour later, I was sitting in an Aeron chair—much easier on the butt than that damn grass tuft—in Quest's fourth floor conference room with the remains of my telephoto lens spread on the table. Jordan, no longer a wolf but still naked and wrapped in one of the silvery space blankets that Zeke kept stocked in the Quest supply closet, was curled up in another comfy chair across from me.

"I'm really sorry, Hugh," he said in a tiny voice, which, if he were still wolfy, would be a pitiful whine. "But I could tell there weren't any dryads in the stinky tree."

I pushed the lens away with a sigh. It was toast. No hope for it at all. "How could you tell?"

He tapped his nose. "Dryads have a specific scent. Wet bark and autumn leaves and sage. The stinky tree didn't have any of those scents." He screwed up his face. "Well, other than the wet bark because I...you know." He pointed at his groin.

"Got it."

He picked at the edge of the blanket. "I'm good at finding things. I've never missed a single one of the Frisbees my little brother buried behind the..." His expression turned furtive. "Never mind." He bit his lip. "But I'm really sorry."

I sighed as Zeke came in with a tea tray, my camera bag slung over his shoulder and the bundle of Jordan's clothing clamped under his arm. "It's okay, Jordan. Clearly the client gave us the wrong information. It's not the first time."

Zeke set the tray on the table, and I noticed it didn't contain only a teapot and cups—it carried two plates of falafel, still steaming gently in what was obviously fresh pita. "I called Bryce—that is, Dr. MacLeod," he said, "and told him what you discovered. He apologized. Apparently he was so annoyed by the client that he didn't bother to investigate whether there might be anything else going on."

I snagged one of the falafel plates. "Not his fault. I mean, we're the investigators. It's kind of our job to figure this stuff out." I took a bite. *Mmmm*. Cumin, coriander, garlic, and lemon. The crunch of lettuce, the sweet acid of a perfectly ripe tomato, the cool tang of tarator sauce. The falafel balls were fluffy and light, not dense and gluey, the pita soft and elastic, not stiff and hard. Perfect. "Thanks for this, Zeke."

He smiled sweetly, the vision spell on his glasses glinting in the halogen ceiling lights. "It's my job to take care of you all. And my pleasure as well."

"Does Dr. MacLeod have any idea what was going on with the dryad confab?"

Zeke shrugged. "He's not sure, but he doesn't believe their attack on you was intentional."

"Looked pretty intentional to me," Jordan mumbled around a mouthful of falafel.

"Well, you did pee on them," I replied. "They might consider that an aggressive act."

Zeke cleared his throat. "I think their, um, charge may have been a reaction to *your* presence, Hugh. Not everyone is aware that you've been vetted by the supe council."

"Provisionally vetted," I grumbled. Although I'd been working with Quest for nearly a year, I was still on probation as far as the supe council was concerned. Some factions continued to object to me knowing as much as I did. They regularly demanded the elimination of what they perceived as a threat to their safety and privacy, and they weren't especially squeamish about ensuring the finality of said elimination. But at least one other faction was trying to use my awareness as proof that the Secrecy Pact had outlived its usefulness and that supes should be free to live in the open at last.

That particular decision wasn't mine, thank goodness, but I'd been allowed into this world, my memories intact, as an active participant rather than an accidental victim in need of therapy or memory adjustments. No way would I ever jeopardize that. I'd been dreaming of this for too long, even if the reverse was not also true: I had yet to run into any supe who harbored dreams of living a human life.

Unfortunately.

I took a gulp of tea, its heat searing my throat. "Are Mal and Niall back yet? I should probably report to them."

"Niall's in his office with the Purl brothers," Zeke said as he gently turned my broken lens in his hands.

"Both the Purls?" Devin and Ronnie Purl were ferret shifters. Devin was a stand-up guy—a low-voltage electrician who worked with both supe and human contractors. Ronnie, though... His ferret instincts were a little too close to the surface. "Did Ronnie get caught with his hands where they shouldn't be again?"

Zeke nodded. "Sadly, yes." He set the lens down carefully. "He was working on one of Devin's crews for a Johnson Construction job. Mr. Johnson's husband stopped by and Ronnie...liberated Mr. Moreau's cashmere overcoat."

I goggled at him. "Ronnie stole from a *vampire*? Is he completely nuts?"

Zeke fussed with the tea tray, nesting the spoons in a precise line. "No. Just desperately attracted to anything soft and cozy. He'd recently snatched a ceremonial cloak from an elemental mage too." His hands shook, and he knocked the spoons out of alignment. Holy crap, he was *nervous*. Almost frightened.

Then I remembered—before the practice was outlawed, mages were known to bind demons into unwilling servitude. It had never happened to Zeke, but it had to his friend AJ, another super sweet demon who now did diagnostic possessions for the supe hospital.

That's right. *Diagnostic possessions*. I'm telling you—this stuff is just *so freaking cool*.

Zeke pointed to the lens. "You can submit an expense report for this, you know, Hugh. It was damaged on the job."

"I know. I will, as soon as I find a replacement." I might need it sooner than I expected if Niall wanted me to tail Ronnie Purl again to keep him out of trouble, but I was picky about my equipment. I took one more bite of my falafel sandwich and stood up. "Thanks again, Zeke. You're the best." I wiped my mouth with the napkin and tossed it in the trash. "I'll finish up later, after I check in with Niall."

Zeke blinked his big, dark eyes. "You don't have to hurry. You're due a break after an entire morning staking out—"

"The wrong tree," Jordan said brightly.

I paused in the doorway. "If I were you, Jordan, I wouldn't harp on that little detail too much. Especially if anybody asks you how you happened to find out it was the wrong tree."

He flushed. "Right. Sorry, Hugh."

I shot him a grin. "No worries. But maybe next time? Don't be so quick to volunteer those particular…forensic services." I studied Jordan's slumped shoulders. "If you're worried I'm going to rat you out to Mal and Niall, don't. I'll keep your involvement vague."

"Thanks, Hugh, but you don't need to cover anything up. I'll tell them myself." He smiled wanly. "Messing up your case is a bigger deal than burying a Frisbee in the back yard, and I'm working on taking responsibility for my screwups."

I lifted a hand in farewell. "In this instance, your screwup exposed a major gap in the client's information, so don't be too hard on yourself."

I took the stairs down to the second floor, where Zeke's reception desk and my bosses' offices were located. But when I entered the lobby, my breath caught in my throat and my heart gave an odd sideways thump.

The room wasn't empty. A huge figure was silhouetted against the window, gazing down into the street. The height, the shaggy hair, the broad shoulders…

"Ted?" I croaked.

The guy whipped around and…he wasn't Ted, although my breath didn't immediately come easier nor my heart settle down. Ted had been married for almost a year and he'd never been mine to begin with. You'd think I'd be over this stupid crush by now, done with harboring the forlorn hope that he'd show up and declare his undying love.

You'd be wrong.

But now that I got a better look at him, this guy wasn't anything like Ted, despite the similar aspect ratio. While Ted's medium brown hair seemed always one week past the need for a haircut, this guy's mane was literally that—shoulder length, with streaks of gold amid the brown. A sort of Jason Momoa-as-Aquaman vibe. His eyes were dark, almost black, instead of Ted's warmer brown, and while Ted's open face was nearly always wreathed in smiles, this guy's clenched jaw could be made of granite. Really grumpy granite. Plus, Ted always brought the scent of the woods and mountains with him. This guy smelled vaguely of fish. *Old* fish.

I pasted on what I hoped was a professional smile. "C-can I help you?"

He narrowed his eyes and gave me the once-over. I was used to that here—all our clients had that first *what the heck?* reaction when they realized I was human. But this guy… His gaze was a little more…focused, if you know what I mean?

"I need to speak to O'Tierney."

*Just shoot me now.* He had a freaking Scottish accent. Ted's American, so that was another difference, but with all the Celtic fae I worked with, I'd become a sucker for the UK accent spectrum, and Scots was my favorite. What can I say? Too much *Outlander* on my solo Netflix nights.

"He's with another client now."

He rolled his eyes. "Kendrick, then, if I must."

I wasn't sure if Mal was with Niall in his meeting with the Purls—he might be off checking with Dr. MacLeod about the feral dryad pack, and once Mal got within ten feet of his husband...well, let's say those meetings tended to be a little extended, if you catch my drift. "I'm not certain—"

"Oh! I'm so sorry. I didn't realize we had a visitor." Zeke bustled in and took his place behind the desk. "Welcome to Quest Investigations. How may we assist you?"

"Bloody hell," the big guy growled. "Stop asking questions, for starters."

Zeke blinked at the man's tone. "I'm sorry, but if we don't ask questions, how will we know what you need?"

The guy glared at Zeke. "You're the demon. Surely you can tell by looking."

Zeke's blush blotched his pale skin. "I don't use that ability here. It would be unprofessional."

Poor Zeke had eons of trying to please totally unpleasable people—the demons who ran Sheol weren't exactly mellow— and it wasn't fair that he had to put up with it from our clients. I squared my shoulders and faced the guy down.

"You've come to our offices, therefore you must need something. It's to your benefit to explain what that something is. We can get all the formalities out of the way, so when Niall and Mal are free, you won't waste any time."

"Any *more* time, you mean," he grumbled.

I gritted my teeth. "Why don't we start with your name?"

He scowled at us from under lowered brows. "Is this a trick question?"

I shared a bewildered glance with Zeke. "It's pretty standard for people who want to engage Quest's services."

He jerked his chin at Zeke. "Tell him."

Zeke sighed. "Sometimes names can be used to bind people against their will. Demons, for instance." He smiled rather thinly. "However, sir, you needn't worry about that here. Our security spells negate any possible misuse of true names."

The guy harrumphed. His shoulders might have relaxed a fraction, although with their width, it was hard to tell. "Brodie," he said. "Lachlan Brodie."

Zeke nodded and typed it into his computer with his usual blinding speed. "Mr. Brodie, could you give us a general idea of the reason you're here today?"

For a moment, Brodie's dark eyes glinted with something that could have been wicked humor. He reached into a small cooler I hadn't noticed next to his feet. "This," he said, and slapped an extremely dead fish in the middle of Zeke's desk.

# CHAPTER THREE

"You could have just explained your problem," I said as I hustled Brodie into the second floor conference room. "You didn't have to contaminate Zeke's desk."

His mouth quirked. "It was wrapped up tight."

"Not tight enough to mask the smell. *Faugh!* I picked it up as soon as I walked into the lobby." Although now that he'd offloaded it onto poor Zeke, Brodie smelled more like the ocean and less like a seafood market at the end of a really hot day.

"You asked why I was here." He strode over and parked an enormous leather pack on the oval oak table. Thankfully, he'd left the cooler in the other room. "Can't help it if you don't like the answer."

I propped my hands on my hips. "You can answer questions without being a total jerk. People do it every day."

He lifted an eyebrow, and I noticed it was bisected by a thin white scar. "Is this how you treat all your clients?"

I winced and scaled back my glare. He had a point, and I had little room for error when it came to client relations, thanks to my probationary status. "Is this how you treat someone who's trying to help you?"

He pinched the bridge of his nose, and his massive chest rose and fell. "Sorry. It's been so long since I've encountered one that it seems I've forgotten how to behave."

"Encountered one of what?"

His wry smile made me blink because it transformed him from a grumpy brick wall into an actual person. "Anyone who's trying to help me."

Okay, if there's one thing that can derail my annoyance, it's finding out somebody's in trouble. I wasn't sure how dead fish translated into trouble—unless it was one of those *Godfather* references which I had *never* been able to follow—but supes were notoriously self-sufficient and nobody came to Quest unless they had a problem they couldn't solve on their own.

I gestured to one end of the table. "Why don't you have a seat? Can I get you anything? Tea? Coffee?"

"Water would be grand." He lowered himself into the specially spelled chair that adjusted to accommodate any client's size.

I pulled a bottle of water out of the room's mini-fridge, and he at least had the grace to nod his thanks when I passed it to him. His salty-ocean-breeze scent tickled my nose again. Since supes tended to wear their nature in their smell as well as in their behavior and appearance, I assumed he was some kind of saltwater-based being. If I had Jordan's nose, I'd probably be able to tell which one, but I didn't, nor was I familiar with all supe flavors. Brodie might be a species I hadn't encountered yet, and a thrill chased across my skin at the notion.

I snagged a legal pad and a pen from the credenza. "What can you tell me about—"

"You're human." His tone was matter of fact rather than accusatory or outraged, a nice change from so many of our clients.

I eyed him warily. "Yes."

"So what *can* I tell you?"

I sighed and pulled my credentials out of my pocket. I slid the laminated card across the table. "Everything."

He studied the card, with its official supe council seal, his eyebrows rising toward his widow's peak. "Impressive." He tossed the card back to me. "That might get you through a few doors, but I'll wager it doesn't make you any more welcome once you're inside."

"I manage," I said stiffly as I tucked the card back in my pocket.

He snorted. "Right. Because the average supe is so welcoming to your lot."

"I suppose *you* are?"

He grinned, his teeth white against his tanned skin. "My kind are *very* welcoming to humans."

"Your kind?" I knew all about the fae's noted penchant for kidnapping humans for their own pleasure, keeping them in Faerie until they tired of them, and then booting them out again. Was Brodie fae? There were a whole raft of fae species, some of them water-based, that I hadn't met. But the King and Queen of Faerie had instituted a zero tolerance no-kidnapping policy, and they were very strict about enforcement.

"He's a bloody selkie." Mal strode in, a scowl on his model-perfect face.

"A selkie?" I sat up straighter because hey, first contact! "Are selkies fae? What's their natural habitat? What do—"

"Later, Hugh." Mal's smile was fond. As a high fae, he was breathtakingly beautiful with his raven black hair and cobalt eyes. As was Niall, for that matter, but neither one of them had ever touched me the way Ted had and still did, hopeless as my feelings were. "Let's find out what the bastard wants first."

Brodie smirked at Mal. "Nice to see you, too, Kendrick. Shagged anybody's fiancé lately?"

I goggled at Mal, who simply strolled to the other end of the table and dropped into a chair, lounging at ease as if he hadn't a care in the world. I guess having regular sex can really relax you.

I wouldn't know.

"First, if somebody *is* engaged, not even I can tell unless he says so. Second, that was years ago. Third"—he waggled his left hand where his platinum wedding band glinted—"I'm a married man, and unlike some, I don't cheat."

Brodie scowled at him. "I never cheated."

"No? Well, maybe not in the bedroom, but pretending you're something you're not counts in my book."

"I wasn't pretending."

"No," Mal drawled, "just left out a few pertinent facts."

Brodie slapped the table. "I didn't come here to discuss ancient history."

Mal's eyes narrowed, and he morphed from indolent to intent in a heartbeat. "Then why *did* you come here?"

"I'd rather speak with O'Tierney."

"Too bad. He's busy. And in any case, we're partners, so I'd find out about it eventually, anyway."

He jerked his chin at me. "And yon human?"

"Hugh's a trusted member of our staff." I warmed a little at Mal's praise. "And since Niall's busy and I can't stand the sight of you, you'll probably be stuck with him, anyway." Okay, warmth gone. "*If* we decide to take your case."

Brodie glowered at Mal—and if everything I'd seen of him so far hadn't convinced me he wasn't like Ted in anything other than size, that look would have done it. Ted would *never* try to incinerate somebody with his eyes.

Then his gaze dropped to his hands where they were fisted on the table top. "I'm being harassed," he grumbled.

"Harassed." Mal's tone was skeptical. "You mean the way you harassed my office manager by slapping a dead herring on his desk?"

"He asked what the problem was, and the herring *is* the problem. That's the third one that's shown up in the last two weeks. The first one was tossed on the deck overnight."

Mal tilted his head, gently swiveling his chair back and forth. "You still have that boat berthed in the Nehalem River?"

Brodie nodded. "And running my charter service." He glanced at me. "Private fishing expeditions. Whale watching. That kind of thing."

I blinked, surprised that he was addressing me. Once Mal or Niall showed up, most clients ignored me. At least when they weren't sneering at me. I bent my head and jotted a note on my pad—even though it was just a doodle of a fish with Xs for eyes —so I wouldn't gape like a total idiot.

"The first time," Brodie continued, "I thought it was just a random thing. Other fishing boats ply the same waters. It could have been an accident."

"Uh huh," Mal said. "Did you keep that first one?"

Brodie screwed up his face. "Hell, no. I tossed it to the gulls. I didn't pay too much attention to it, if you want the truth."

"Then what?"

"It happened again. Another dead herring, only this time, it couldn't have been accidental. It wasn't just tossed on the deck. It was shoved inside the aft locker. I had to replace half my life vests."

Mal studied him, eyes narrowed. "I'd think you'd have found it before it had a chance to...contaminate the equipment."

"I would have, if I hadn't been away for three days scouting the best deepwater sites for an upcoming salmon fishing charter."

I looked up from my pad. "Hold on. How could you scout the ocean without your boat?"

"Selkie," he said, as if that explained everything.

Mal took pity on me. "Selkies are seal shifters."

"Ah." I scribbled more notes, this time more to the point.

Mal gave me a nod of approval. He seemed to be taking this seriously now. *Score!* We might actually have a case that didn't involve me sitting on my butt staring through my camera for a change. "Was that where the odiferous specimen you gifted Zeke with came from?" he asked.

"No. That one showed up this morning. On my engine block. If I hadn't noticed it before I started up, I'd have never gotten rid of the stink." He ran his big hands through his hair. "This is destroying my business. I had to cancel two charters, one after the second attack, and one today. The last thing landlockers need on the open ocean, especially when there's a lot of chop like today, is something else to unsettle their stomachs."

Mal steepled his fingers. "Do you have any idea who might be targeting you?"

"I do." Brodie's expression turned grim. Well, grimmer, since he hadn't exactly been a Cheerful Charlie so far. "I think it's my husband."

My stomach jolted like I was the one on a wave-tossed boat. *Husband.* For the love of Mike, why were all the men around me already taken? Not that Brodie would have been a romantic possibility for me, anyway. Other than his size, he was the exact opposite of the man who unknowingly held my heart.

I cleared my throat. "Why would your husband threaten your livelihood? Surely it affects him too."

Brodie snorted. "You'd think."

"If I remember the man correctly..." Mal tipped his chair back on its gimbals. "...I'd guess he expected a slightly different lifestyle when he accepted your proposal."

"I didn't hide anything from him. He knew the situation. And my reasons."

"Ah, but hope springs eternal, and all that. If I recall his rather fanboyish pillow talk—"

"Oi. None of that," Brodie growled.

"Wait." I held up my hand. "That stuff about fiancés wasn't just generic? You slept with *his* fiancé?"

Mal shot me an irritated look. "Wyn wasn't anybody's fiancé at the time, not yet. Trust me"—Brodie snorted again, earning a glare from Mal—"if I'd known that's what he was looking for, I'd never have taken him out of that damn club." He smirked.

"It's not like I needed to work that hard for partners back in the day."

"So modest," I murmured with an eye roll, earning a grin from my boss and a glance of grudging approval from Brodie.

"Just stating the facts. The Wyn I met was something of a celebrity hound. A status seeker. I wasn't nearly important enough for him, thank the Goddess."

I frowned, glancing between the big, rough-hewn man—selkie, I guess—and Mal with his nearly surreal beauty. Yes, Brodie was attractive, especially given my predilection for large hairy men, but Mal was…Mal. He would have been the Queen's Enforcer back then, hardly somebody to sneeze at, even though he'd had a terrible reputation as a serial dater at the time. But surely a status seeker would have found the challenge nearly irresistible.

"If that's all you saw in Wyn," Brodie said tiredly, "you didn't know him as well as you think."

"I saw enough to keep the connection brief," Mal retorted. "So why do you think he's stinking up your boat?"

Brodie heaved a sigh. "We're severing the knot."

"Severing the knot?" I asked, glancing from Brodie to Mal.

Mal waggled his ring finger again. "Bryce and I got married at city hall after we had our handfasting in Faerie. Wyn's fae, and since selkies have Faerie reciprocity, they'd be eligible for a Faerie ceremony." He glanced at Brodie. "I'm assuming you never jumped through the Outer World legal hoops?" Brodie shook his head, and Mal turned to me again. "So in order to end their marriage, all they need to do is sever the knot in Faerie. It's called a sundering ceremony." He flicked his fingers. "No pesky Outer World legal shenanigans necessary, although it does require royal dispensation."

Brodie shrugged. "It was taking a wee bit more time to arrange the sundering than we'd imagined."

"Dragging your feet?" Mal's tone wasn't entirely unsympathetic.

"It's not a step to take lightly," Brodie said defensively. "There were…complications. I…wanted to make certain it was best for him. For both of us."

"Do you think he's lashing out? Retaliating for the delay?" Mal asked.

From Brodie's expression, *he* wanted to lash out at Mal's apparent insult to his husband. *Must be still in love with him, I guess.* Especially if he was trying for a reconciliation. "I'd heard…" He took a gulp of his water. "I think he's seeing his old bloke. The one he left for me."

Mal choked on a laugh. "Reid Martinson? That wanker? With a blow *that* low, surely you were tempted to respond with a little dalliance of your own?"

He glowered at Mal from under lowered eyebrows. "I made a promise, and when I make a promise, I keep it."

Something was tugging at my memory. Martinson… Martinson… *Aha!* "Isn't Martinson the name of that elemental mage who lives in the West Hills?"

Mal nodded briefly. "That's Pierce Martinson, Reid's father. Reid is magic-null, but makes up for it with all the money he's rolling in."

"Bloody entitled git," Brodie growled. "His daddy's been enabling him since his cradle. They never stopped poking at Wyn the whole time we were married. Probably why he…" He shook his head, jaw tightening. "I don't blame him. He expected more from our mating than he got. He was tired of waiting for me to…to…"

"To give up the boat?" I asked.

He turned his scowl on me. "To take the bloody throne."

My eyes widened, and I glanced from him to Mal. "Throne? What throne?"

Mal chuckled. "What Mr. Brodie failed to mention is that he's king of the selkies. Or he would be if he ever stepped up to the plate and accepted his responsibilities."

*King of the selkies*. Good grief. And I thought Ted was way out of my league. Not that I was thinking about Lachlan Brodie in the same way. Mostly. But holy crap. King of the selkies?

"That's a load of bollocks," Brodie growled. "We don't need a bloody king. This isn't the Middle Ages."

"Nevertheless, didn't Wyn sign on expecting to become a prince?"

Brodie scrubbed his hands over his face. "Look. I never promised him anything other than faithfulness and all my worldly goods."

"Seems like a lot," I said faintly. It would certainly be enough for me.

"Except Wyn had a rather different notion of what a selkie king's worldly goods entailed," Mal said dryly. "Wonder where he got those ideas?"

Brodie glared at him. "Not from me. Somebody filled his head with tales about an *undersea palace*." His tone dripped with disgust. "Bunch of codswallop put about by my ancestors to impress the human women they wanted to seduce. But he'd seen my boat. He'd even gone on a couple of charters with me, seen how things worked. I'd taken him out in my skin—"

"You do *naked* charters?" I croaked. Just the thought of it... Well, in Oregon, it might be a little chilly, but—

"Mind out of the gutter, Hugh. He means in his seal skin," Mal said with a smirk. "He took him on a swim in shifted form. Selkies can do that and keep their mate safe underwater."

I shivered a little at that. The Pacific, even in the summer, wasn't exactly bathwater-toasty off the Oregon coast. "*Brrr*."

Brodie's mouth curved in a half smile and for a minute my brain winked offline because...wow. "We selkies know how to keep our lovers warm, lad, never fear."

Okay, was that flirty? Or just factual? Ugh, he was *married*. I swallowed thickly. "Right. Guess I've got some research to do." I blinked when his smile grew. "I mean *online* research. Or libraries. Books. And articles. And..." I slumped in my seat, studiously ignoring Mal's grin of unholy glee. "I'll just be quiet now."

Luckily for my terminal blush, Zeke bustled in with the tea tray. He gave Brodie a wary glance and approached him slowly, probably checking for more weaponized fish. He started to slide the tray onto the table at Brodie's elbow, but the pack was in his way. He reached out to move it aside.

"No!" Brodie leaped out of his chair, sending it spinning away on its well-oiled casters to bang against the wall. He snatched up the bag and clutched it to his chest, glaring at a wide-eyed Zeke. "Touch that again and I'll take your bloody hand off."

# CHAPTER FOUR

"I-I'm sorry, sir," Zeke murmured. "I didn't mean—"

"Stand down, Brodie, you arsehole." Mal patted Zeke's shoulder. "Don't mind him, boyo. He's a mite tetchy about his little satchel." Mal jerked his chin at Brodie, whose chest was heaving in a *very* distracting way. "Got your skin in there, do you?"

My pen fell from my suddenly numb fingers. "S-skin?"

"Ah, bugger." Brodie wiped one hand over his face, the other arm still clenched around his pack. "Sorry, lad," he said to Zeke with a grimace. "And sorry about the fish earlier. I'll clean it up."

Zeke smiled shakily. "No need, sir. I've already taken care of it." He glanced at Mal. "If there's nothing else?"

"Nah. It's all good. Thanks, mate."

Zeke hustled out of the room as if his feet were on fire—and considering he'd lived in Sheol for most of his centuries-long life, he probably knew exactly how that felt.

Mal stared pointedly at Brodie until he retrieved his chair and sat down again, the pack in his lap. "Now. Suppose you tell us the whole story. Starting with why in all the bloody hells you're carrying your skin around in a fecking knapsack?"

Brodie hunched over the pack. "I had a little...disagreement with the coastal witches' collective. Until I get it sorted, they've rescinded the protection spells on the boat. I can't risk leaving my skin there."

Mal snorted. "If your boat's physically accessible for the first time, no wonder you're getting bombarded with the world's smelliest catch. You've probably pissed off any number of people who'd like to smack you with a sturgeon."

"They were herrings."

"Whatever. The point is your winning personality hasn't endeared you to many." Mal lifted an eyebrow. "Or any, for that matter. What makes you think Wyn's responsible?"

"Because the first one didn't show up until I told him the sundering would have to wait until we had a counseling session with your brother."

I jotted another note. "Couple's therapy?" In addition to being the Faerie Queen's champion, Mal's brother, Dr. Alun Kendrick, was a psychologist serving the supe community. "Was that your way of trying to work things out?"

"Not my idea," Brodie replied. "It's a new requirement Their Majesties have put in place." He wrinkled his nose. "They claim they want to give their subjects tools, options, and support. We could have agreed to waive it, but I...wouldn't."

"Why did you refuse?" I blurted. I half expected Brodie to ignore me. A lot of our clients did—they didn't feel like they owed a human anything, not even courtesy. But he actually looked...embarrassed?

"Talking with Dr. Kendrick seemed little enough to ask for a step this final. I made a promise when we wed that I'd be with Wyn forever, care for him forever."

*Did you promise to love him forever?* A guy that big could do some damage to a vulnerable partner, and if he was angry about the split—and about the cheating—he could be setting Wyn up. Because Brodie didn't seem like he was particularly heartbroken. Although maybe he could hide his heart really well under all those muscles.

I tore my gaze away from his face before I could see the answer to my question and scanned my notes. I started to sketch out a timeline. "When Wyn asked for the divorce—I mean, the sundering—was that the first inkling you'd had that he was unhappy in the marriage?"

The silence after the question was louder than a shout. I glanced up to find Brodie scowling fiercely at the table.

Mal gave me a *seriously, dude?* look. "I believe the first inkling was when he cheated with Reid Martinson."

I winced. "Ah. Right. Um…when was that?"

Brodie heaved a sigh. "Right after the solstice. Pierce Martinson hosted a big party at his house for the holiday. We were invited, but I had a five-day charter scheduled. Wyn was supposed to crew for me. He wanted me to cancel the booking, kept staring all moony-eyed at the invitation as if it had come from the Queen herself, but we needed the money. We had a big fight." He glanced up at me from under lowered brows. "He may have brought up his disappointment that a king was living like a peasant."

I stabbed my pen into the paper with a little more force than necessary. I was starting to get a very unflattering picture of Wyn. A marriage is supposed to be a partnership. Why didn't the whiner help instead of throwing guilt around and making Lachlan feel like a failure?

*Lachlan.* So now my mind was on a first name basis with him? I needed to get a freaking grip. He was *married.* He was a supe. And he may or may not be a manipulative user, so there was that.

I clutched my pen harder and schooled my voice into what I hoped was a neutral tone. "What happened then?"

"I…apologized."

*Grrr.* "For what?"

"For not being able to give him what he needed. What he deserved."

*I'll tell you what he deserved. A quick kick in the pants.* "Did he apologize to you?"

Lachlan's eyebrows reached for his hairline. "Why would he?"

"Because he— Never mind. Did you cancel the booking?"

"I couldn't. Not without penalty, and like I said, we needed the money. But I told Wyn he could stay ashore and go to the party if he wanted."

I almost didn't need to hear what happened next. I could guess. Little Lord Whiner toddles off to the fancy party in the big mansion and sees the life he *could* be leading if he wasn't tied to a hardworking guy with no ambition for anything more than a decent life. It probably wouldn't have been tough for Reid to get into his pants, no kicking required.

But if I wanted to make the jump from surveillance to full investigator, I needed to ask the hard questions. "Is that when Wyn slept with Reid?"

Lachlan nodded morosely. "The first time. He confessed at once. Said he wasn't even sure why he'd done it and promised it wouldn't happen again."

"But it did," I said gently.

Another nod. "The summer was busy. Business was great. I was able to start putting aside some money to take Wyn away for our anniversary, but it meant I was gone almost constantly. When I was ashore, he was so angry that he wouldn't even kiss me. I didn't have the energy to fight, so I mostly slept on the boat."

I had a hard time picturing the idiot who'd refuse to kiss Lachlan Brodie, but then I was the guy who'd been in love with a grizzly shifter for years, so I can't exactly pass judgment on anyone's romantic faux pas. "Were the security spells still in place then?"

He nodded. "I'd left my skin on the boat when I got back from my Labor Day booking. I'd brought back a net of mussels from the trip, since Wyn always liked those. I was going to surprise him with the vacation news. But when I got home, he wasn't there." He swallowed, and sorrow flickered across his face. This wasn't a man who was angry about his partner's betrayal. He might not be totally heartbroken, but he was definitely saddened. "I figured he was just out for a bit. The gym. Maybe one of the lakes."

"Wait a sec. He refused to sail on the ocean with you, but he'll hang out at a lake?" I must not have kept the outrage out of my tone, because Mal cut in smoothly.

"Wyn is a Corlun Dwr."

Another one I hadn't heard of. I sighed happily. Sometimes, I loved my job. "And that is…"

"Welsh water sprite." Mal tilted an eyebrow at Brodie. "Fresh water. Not salt. To be honest, I was surprised at his original enthusiasm for, shall we say, a brackish union."

"Don't be an arse, Kendrick," Lachlan growled.

Mal grinned wolfishly. "Sorry. But two millennia of practice makes that an impossibility. At least that's what my husband says." He winced, probably from the obvious fondness in his tone when he mentioned his own happy marriage. "Sorry. Carry on."

"He showed up later, a little tipsy but not completely drunk." He swallowed. "Reid was with him. They were half undressed before they realized I was in the kitchen."

I grimaced. "Ouch."

"Wyn didn't even try to excuse himself. With that bastard Reid smirking at me over Wyn's shoulder in my own blasted living room, Wyn demanded a sundering. Of course I said no."

"Um…" I screwed up my face. "If you don't mind my asking…why?"

"Why what?"

"Why say no? You had the evidence of his cheating right there, smirking at you. Why not cut your losses?"

He glared at me. "Because I made a *promise*. Just because he broke his doesn't release me from mine. We needed to talk about it."

"And did you?"

He snorted. "No. Reid left, but Wyn just kept repeating that he wanted the sundering. It was like he only knew the same dozen words. I decided to let him cool off a bit, so I told him he could have the apartment and I'd stay on the boat until he was ready to talk. When I got back to the boat, though, the magistra was already there, unwinding the security spells."

"Why?"

"She claims the collective had a complaint against me for violating natural consequences by luring fish to the boat for my charters."

"Did you?"

He glared at me, clearly outraged. "No, I bloody well didn't. That's totally against my principles." He finally plonked the bag back on the table, rattling the unused teacups. "It was Reid. Had to be."

"Well," Mal drawled, "he certainly has the money and the spite to do it, not to mention access to his father's bloody strong magic and influence. But would the collective act on it without a thorough investigation? Assessing an inappropriate penalty just invites a big fat natural consequence to fall on their head."

"With enough money," Lachlan said morosely, "anyone can be subverted. Even a witches' collective. Even the supe high council."

"Watch yourself, mate," Mal said, his tone laced with warning. "Let's not go making wild accusations. Not in front of me, anyway, seeing as how I answer to the high council."

Lachlan fixed Mal with a steady stare. "Are you saying the council is incorruptible?"

"Hells, no. I've learned the hard way that everybody's got their own breaking point. But you need something other than insinuation to make that kind of thing stick, so let's focus on the more local issue. Let's assume that Reid found the right leverage, or that your stellar past behavior made it easy for the magistra to believe the charges. She removed the spells. Carry on."

"The next day's when the first..." He made a rolling gesture with one hand as if he were looking for a good description.

"Fish flinging?" I said helpfully, although considering the fulminating glance Lachlan threw me, he didn't appreciate my attempt to lighten the situation.

"Yes," he growled. "When Wyn tossed the herring onto the deck—"

"Hold on a mo," Mal said. "Wyn's a Seelie fae. Granted, since Seelie and Unseelie are one big dysfunctional family now, things are a tad different, but this isn't the kind of behavior the Seelie engage in. And Wyn's a water sprite. They have a steward's relationship with all creatures who dwell beneath the waves, blah blah blah. Why would he entice a herring into his net just to heave it onto your boat to make a point, especially since the Pacific herring population isn't exactly burgeoning these days? How do you know it was him?"

Lachlan hunched further into himself. "A friend on the dock saw him."

Mal's eyes narrowed. "And you trust this friend?"

Lachlan nodded. "They'd have no reason to lie. They watch out for me, same as I do for them."

Mal took a deep breath. "Grand. We've got a Welsh fae acting out of character and a witches' collective risking a divine retribution from the Triple Goddess for defying natural consequences. Bloody hells, mate, who did you piss off?"

# CHAPTER
## FIVE

"Will you take the case or not?" Lachlan asked, not a speck of pleading—or hope—in his tone. Clearly, he expected Mal to turn him down.

Mal tapped his steepled fingers against his lips, his eyes narrowed as he glanced between Lachlan and me. Alarm crept down my spine like phantom spiders. When Mal got that look, it didn't bode well for somebody—I just wasn't entirely sure *who* that somebody was.

"Quest Investigations will take the case—"

"Thank the Goddess," Lachlan muttered.

"But there are conditions."

He gave Mal a disgusted look. "Why am I not surprised? With you, there's always a catch."

"Funny," Mal said with a grin, "that's what I always say about druids. But you know what I've found?" He leaned forward and jabbed a finger at Lachlan. "Sometimes getting caught is the best thing that can happen to you."

Lachlan paired his eye-roll with a long-suffering sigh. "Fine. What are your conditions?"

Mal's gaze slid to me. "As it happens, Niall's unavailable right now for reasons I can't go into." He assumed an expression that I'm sure he thought was earnest and reliable, but the glint in his eye was a dead giveaway. He needed to take lessons from Zeke. "Privileged client information. You understand."

"Naturally." For a water-natured being, Lachlan could sure dial up the dry comments.

"Hugh will take the lead on this. He'll accompany you back to the boat and scope out the crime scene."

I sat up straighter. A case of my own? One that wasn't 100% surveillance? *Yes!*

Lachlan frowned. "What about Wyn? Aren't we going to question him?"

"*We* are not," Mal said, smirking when Lachlan bristled. "However, *I* am. You will not be present."

"But—"

"Have you had much luck with him yet?"

"No," Lachlan said sulkily.

"If you were there, you'd probably stick your big flipper in your mouth as normal. Wyn will be more likely to open up to another Welsh fae when a stroppy selkie isn't glaring at him from the corner."

"Fine," he grumbled.

"Excellent." Mal slapped his hands on the table and stood. "Hugh, can I speak with you outside for a moment?"

I scrambled out of my chair while Lachlan peered at both of us through narrowed eyes. "Secrets already?"

"Not about you." Mal grinned. "Well, mostly. Drink some tea. Eat a scone. Try not to terrorize the staff."

I followed Mal into the corridor. Once the door was closed, his cocky grin disappeared and his forehead wrinkled in very uncharacteristic worry. I glanced at the closed door. "Is there something about this case that I—"

"No!" Mal huffed a breath. "Sorry, mate. It's just that their royal fae majesties have gotten their knickers in a twist because we've not found any of the Disappeared, which was the whole reason for this company's existence."

I frowned. "You're still looking, though." I didn't have to ask. I knew. Niall spent more time than his bard boyfriend appreciated tracking down leads with his prior contacts among the sketchier Unseelie fae. Mal and his druid husband did the same on the Seelie side. "It's not as though we haven't solved other cases."

He ran his hands through his hair. If I'd done that, I'd have looked like a scarecrow coming off a three-day bender. Mal just looked charmingly tousled. "I know. But we're heading on toward Calan Gaeaf."

I translated—Calan Gaeaf equaled Samhain equaled Halloween, more or less. "So?"

"So any fae who've been making their way in the Outer World with no help from the court or contact with Faerie would have had a tough road and might have...let's say strayed from the straight and narrow? Herne and his pack of Cwn Annwn ride out that night on the Wild Hunt, seeking their rightful prey in traitors, oath-breakers, and conspirators. Herne isn't a particularly discerning bloke and his hounds take their cue from him." Mal winced. "Not one to quibble over gray areas, Herne isn't, and any fae who's skirted the law might be caught in his net."

I swallowed. "Got it." I wondered if the feral dryads from this morning would be in danger. There was still a lot about supe law that I didn't understand.

"Anyway, we've got Ronnie Purl sorted. He's doing community service to compensate for his light-fingered escapades."

I blinked. "Community service? Like picking up trash along the highway?"

Mal laughed. "Not *human* community service. *Supe* community service."

"What kind of community service would he do for a vampire?" It didn't really bear thinking about, although I knew that since he and Rusty got married, Casimir didn't use any living human blood hosts. There was a, er, sexual component to feeding, and Casimir was nothing if not faithful to his husband.

Mal waved one hand as if batting my words away. "Not Cas. He doesn't care, as long as he gets his coat back. Ronnie's other victim demanded a bit more than the return of stolen property, however, so he's working off his debt with twenty hours of volunteer labor." Mal snorted. "As it happens, I'll be able to check in on him. His other target was Pierce Martinson." Mal grinned wryly. "Not the smartest tool in the shed, our Ronnie. When he's scampering about pilfering pretties, he should aim at more forgiving blokes like Cas."

I frowned at that. "So only nice people should be crime victims?"

"Goddess, no. Nobody should be a victim. All I'm saying is witches aren't the only ones who should worry about natural consequences." Mal's smile turned into a wince. "Anyway, sorry to saddle you with yon grumpy git."

"I don't mind." I couldn't stop my own grin. "It's my first solo case that's not just surveillance." My grin faded. "Isn't it?"

Mal waggled his hand. "Yes and no. I'm not convinced there's much going on other than malicious misdemeanors. There may not be anything to discover since Wyn was spotted that first time."

My heart sank. "So this is a non-case?"

"Maybe. But it'll give you practice documenting a crime scene even if it's irrelevant. Think you're up for it?" He peered at me, no doubt picking up on my disappointment. "If you'd rather not—"

"No! I mean, yes. I want the chance. Even if Lachlan doesn't want to press charges, he's owed the truth and an apology, at the very least. Just because he's a big man doesn't mean he can't be hurt."

Mal tilted his head, his blue eyes shrewd. "He's not Ted, mate," he said gently.

Shame made my beard itch. Did everybody know about my crush on Ted? Well. Yes. They did. Because I'd admitted it in open court while under the Queen's truth spell. "I know. But he still deserves justice."

"Just don't go giving him more credit than he deserves for decency." Mal rubbed the back of his head. "I'm not sure he's got much. Although you might have a care."

"A care about what?"

Mal's grin took on its usual wicked glint. "Unleash your nosy parker superpowers on selkies and you'll find out. Back in the day, his sort were known to be especially irresistible to humans. Although the only thing I find irresistible about him is the irresistible urge to kick him in the arse." He strode off down the hall.

Irresistible? Was *that* why I kept having inappropriate reactions to him? Not because he reminded me of Ted, but because of his species characteristics? Clearly I had some research ahead of me.

And no, not the hands-on kind of research. Or lips-on. Or— Gah!

I raced upstairs to fetch my gear from the fourth floor conference room. Jordan was gone, the silvery blanket folded neatly in his chair. I sighed at the remains of my telephoto lens. If I was documenting the scene at close quarters, I wouldn't need it, but I hated to be without my full kit. I grabbed my camera bag and jacket and ran back down to the second floor.

When I walked back into the room, Lachlan was slumped in his chair, a scone in his hand, although he seemed to be crumbling it onto the plate rather than eating it.

"So," I said brightly, and then winced at my tone. I wasn't a Disney tour guide, for crying out loud. "Are you ready to head back to your boat?"

He nodded glumly and stood, slinging his pack over one shoulder. "Might as well get it over with."

I'd like to say that wasn't the usual attitude of any man when faced with spending time with me, but I'd be lying. My smile turned into a clenched-teeth grimace. "You're out at Nehalem Bay, didn't you say? There's a regular FTA stop above Dewton, not far from where I live. We can pick up my car there—"

He scowled at me. "FTA?"

"Fae Transportation Association."

"Never heard of it."

"The new king started it as a way to give fae new employment opportunities." I pulled one of the bespelled oak leaves from my pocket. Sheesh, it was starting to crumble around the edges. I needed to check in with Zeke and get a new supply. I was running low anyway. "One of them will escort us through Faerie. Saves a lot of time. That's how I commute to work every day."

He shook his head, sending his long hair flying. "Not bloody likely. I'm not about to dodge through Faerie, beholden to some supercilious git like Mal Kendrick."

"Mal isn't—" I cut off my indignant reply. Clearly Lachlan and Mal had history, and if I'd learned anything in my year with the supes, it was that stepping into old feuds was never a good idea. Besides, I only had another two months to go before my probationary year was up and I didn't want to jeopardize it by antagonizing a client, especially my first solo—more or less —client.

Who attracted me more than I wanted to admit, thanks no doubt to his selkie mojo. But that was magic for you—cool, but also inconvenient.

"It would more likely be a duergar, a trow, or—" I remembered Jordan's illicitly upgraded app. Was that in use by anybody other than him and his werewolf friends? "Well, not one of the high fae, anyway."

Lachlan snorted. "Too good to toddle about with the likes of us, are they?"

I wanted to argue, but he had a point. Some of the high fae were still in denial about the news that "high" and "greater" didn't mean "better." It just meant *taller* and/or *larger*. "It's really the most efficient way to travel."

"Maybe yes, maybe no. But I'm not doing it. Besides, my truck is parked down the street. I'm not about to leave it here."

I sighed. Looked like I was in for an uncomfortable couple of hours in close proximity to Lachlan. I couldn't very well just say I'd meet him there. I had no idea where *there* was. Besides, he was my client. I could use the drive to find out more about the case.

I wasn't thinking about learning more about *him*. No. Of course not.

As I followed him down the stairs and onto the Pearl District sidewalk—*not* perving on his shoulders or his butt, even though they were *right there*—I was intensely grateful that I wasn't still under that lousy truth spell.

Because if I was, I couldn't keep lying to myself.

# CHAPTER SIX

I needn't have worried about exposing my inappropriate attraction during the drive, because by the time we were halfway to the Coast Range, Lachlan hadn't spoken more than a dozen words to me, despite my attempts to initiate conversation. I finally gave up, pulled out my phone, and used the time to research selkies.

I sent a couple of emails—one to Dr. MacLeod, who, as a druid, was actually *supposed* to know this stuff, and one to Tanner Araya, a young werewolf who was Dr. MacLeod's student and unofficial assistant. Tanner was helping Dr. MacLeod trace the history of supernatural species from original source documents and interviews.

Both of them responded almost at once, Dr. MacLeod because he was just that efficient, and Tanner because he was so freaking excited about his project and loved talking about it.

From what they said, most of the commonly accepted lore about selkies wasn't too far off the truth. However, Mal's warning to me about their attraction for humans—and vice versa—differed vastly by gender on both sides of the species line.

It seemed a female selkie was far more likely to be the victim of a human man who stole her seal skin and forced her into unwilling wifehood. The instant she found her skin, though—

often through unwitting assistance from her children—she was out of there.

On the other hand, in stories with male selkies and human women, the human actually *chose* to initiate, er, contact as well as maintain it. Although the resulting relationship tended to be nurturing and mutually agreeable, the male selkie didn't spend a lot of time on land and never made any promise that he would, which the human woman appeared to either accept or else blithely ignore during the courtship phase. However, he never coerced her by anything other than his personal charm and attractiveness.

I glanced sidelong at Lachlan. Attractiveness? Oh, yeah. Charm? Not so much.

The truck started the climb up the Coast Range, so I hurriedly clicked on another of Tanner's links before I lost the cell signal.

"What's your name again?" Lachlan asked.

"Matt," I said absently, absorbed in another selkie tale.

"Matt? That's not what Kendrick called you."

My head shot up at the growly suspicion in Lachlan's tone, and I realized what I'd said. Heat rushed up my throat. This was my first solo case, and I couldn't even remember to give the client a consistent name. Way to build trust.

"No. He calls me Hugh. It's kind of a joke. When I first started working for Quest, our clients kept referring to me as *the human*. Mal started calling me Hugh just to back them into a name rather than an epithet. My real name is Matthew. Matt. Matt Steinitz. But you can call me Hugh."

"Bollocks to that," Lachlan growled. "Your name's Matthew, so that's what I'll call you."

I wanted to protest—I kind of liked having the demarcation between my old life where I only dreamed of supernatural beings and my new life where I was surrounded by them. Besides, only Ted called me Matt, and I wasn't sure I wanted to blur that line any further. But the way Lachlan pronounced

*Matthew* sounded almost like he was smooshing both names together: *MattHugh*.

I guessed I could handle it.

"All right." My voice was a little gruff. "Did you have a question?"

"If you work for Kendrick and O'Tierney in Portland, why are you living in Dewton? Bit more than a wee commute, isn't it?"

I patted my jacket pocket. "I use the FTA. Besides, a lot of my assignments are surveillance"—all of them actually, until now—"which could be anywhere. I've got a regular FTA driver now. A duergar."

"Duergar?" Was that admiration in Lachlan's tone? "Wasn't aware they did anything other than drink and brawl."

"Things have changed. Frang's a good guy. We've arranged a time for him to show up at the spot I told you about in the hills above the town each morning." It was outside a cave Ted used to shift in before he got married, in the days when he and I had breakfast together regularly. "I bring him doughnuts from the diner and he never sneers at me for being human."

Lachlan snorted. "Not a very high bar, that, is it, lad?"

"It's not one many are willing to clear," I said ruefully. "In fact, I'm not sure most supes realize the bar even exists."

"And *that*," Lachlan said as we rolled into Dewton, "is why I live where I do. Shirking my royal responsibilities." I could practically hear the air quotes in his tone. "Bloody supes need to get over themselves and accept that the world has changed."

I swiveled, leaning against the window so I could look at him, his big hands competent on the steering wheel, his gaze sharp as he slowed down to drive through town.

"But isn't that why you *should* interact with your...your subjects more? What if they need help? I mean, sure, some of the supes I've met have been jerks, but not all humans are exactly prizes either."

He glanced at me, his lips quirked in a smile, and my heart did another weird sideways hop. "Never said they were." He returned his attention to the road. "Everybody's got the potential to be an arse, lad, and most folks are willing to live up to it in full."

"But shouldn't you give them the benefit of the doubt? Doesn't everybody have the potential to be good, too?"

Lachlan headed out of Dewton—it wasn't that big—and toward the turnoff to Nehalem Bay. "Are you one of those glass-half-full blokes? Because in my experience, the glass is bloody empty most of the time."

Wow. If anything could prove to me that Lachlan wasn't Ted, that statement did it. I'm not sure Ted believes a person could be anything other than confused, let alone downright evil. Apparently Lachlan had the opposite view. Although...

"When you say the glass is empty, do you mean you think people are inherently evil? That being good is the exception rather than the rule?"

He turned onto the road that led around the bay, toward the docks along the river. "I don't think people are inherently anything. Except lazy, perhaps. If it's easy for them to be good, then they'll give it a go. But as soon as it gets hard, they'll let all those fine intentions slide in favor of expediency. Their own good will always trump the good of anyone else."

I squirmed a little in my seat. Back when I was still working for the tabloids, either as an employee or later as a freelancer, I'd sold photographs that could have endangered the supernatural community. Heck, I could have endangered *Ted*, since half of the shots were of him in partial shift. I'd profited from those pictures, but that was almost incidental.

I'd taken them—I'd *pursued* them—because I wanted them to be true. For the existence, the *wonder* of magic to be true. Did that mean my own good trumped the good of supes who were trying to fly under the radar? Or of Ted, who'd only wanted a friend?

Sure, I was working *for* them now, but most of the community still treated me like I might explode at any moment, turn informant, and blast the news of their lives across the world. That's why I was still on probation after almost a year. That's why the hardliners on the council had insisted my camera had to be bespelled, so I wouldn't be able to offer any revealing shots to my former employers.

Oh, yeah. Didn't I mention that? Another reason why I couldn't buy just *any* telephoto lens to replace the one that got dryadified was that it had to work with the restrictive spells on my equipment. Try to attach one that wasn't up to the strain and it melted.

Ask me how I know.

But what none of them understood, apparently, was that this world, the hidden world, the hidden *people, mattered* to me. Even if I'd never be one of them, never truly belong, knowing that they existed was all I'd ever dreamed of.

I sighed. I just wish it felt like *enough*.

"So, do you think..." I trailed off, because Lachlan obviously wasn't listening to me. Eyes narrowed, he was peering out the windshield at a small figure in a rainbow beanie and an oversized canvas coat in army green who huddled at the end of a dock where a big old-fashioned cabin cruiser was moored at the farthest slip. "Is that your boat?"

He didn't reply, just pulled into a spot a good thirty feet away from the boat, even though there was an open place right in front of it, and threw the truck into park. He opened the door at the same time that he turned off the ignition and leaped out, practically sprinting toward the figure.

I struggled with my seatbelt, cursing when it wouldn't release right away. Was that Wyn? Their grunge chic didn't exactly fit Mal's description of Wyn's upscale sensibilities.

I squinted through the bug-splattered windshield. I had no idea how large a Corlun Dwr was, but this person was about half Lachlan's size. Mal had called Lachlan *stroppy*. Did that translate to violence? If he attacked Wyn—if this *was* Wyn—it wouldn't do his case any good, and I'd be responsible.

I didn't want anyone to get hurt on my watch. Not Lachlan, and not Wyn, even if he was sending anti-love notes to his husband in the form of deceased sea life.

I finally managed to free myself from the seatbelt and practically fell off the cliff that was Lachlan's truck, barely avoiding taking a header onto the buckled pavement. I raced for the dock, but as I got closer and got a good look at the other person, I realized they weren't adult. True, a lot of supes looked no different from humans, but I'd never seen one who looked like a tweenager before.

Yeah, I'd seen college-age werewolves, and my friend David, who's married to Mal's brother, Dr. Kendrick—and is himself a magical healer, if you can believe that—told me his husband treats some younger supes, including the seven-year-old dragon shifter prince. But the community tended to close ranks around the young of all species—that's why I'd nearly gotten lunched by the supe council for pictures of the supe elementary school that I didn't even take—so I doubted a supe youngster would be wandering around on their own out here. Ergo, they must be as human as I was.

Lachlan, for a change, didn't loom like a madrone full of feral dryads. It was weird. His whole aspect had changed. The way he held his shoulders—down and curved forward. The expression on his face—soft and concerned. The way he positioned himself—blocking the chilly wind off the ocean so the kid was safe in his lee.

Well. Five minutes ago I'd never have believed such a miraculous metamorphosis was possible, and I'd seen a hillside transform into animate mud monsters.

When I came staggering up, puffing a little because I really needed to up my fitness regime, the kid shrank away from me and into Lachlan's side. Okay, so I might look a little deranged, considering I'd been goggling at Lachlan like he'd just sprouted a second head—something I hadn't seen, but Zeke assured me was quite common in Sheol, the demon realm. Even so, I wasn't exactly an imposing specimen. Mid-thirties, a little soft in the middle, not too tall. Nondescript brown hair and beard, although I tried to keep them neatly trimmed.

On the other hand, white male privilege was a thing, as was the power imbalance between adult and child, and the kid didn't know me from Beelzebub. I stepped back and glanced up at Lachlan. "Everything okay?"

"Grand." He draped an arm across the kid's shoulder. "Blair, this is Matthew. A...friend."

Well, *that* was noncommittal. Guess Lachlan didn't want Blair to know that I was a professional snoop.

Blair's pointed chin wobbled as they looked me up and down through overlong brown bangs mashed against their forehead by the rainbow beanie. Their gaze didn't move above my neck, as though they were afraid to meet my eyes.

I held still, my arms loose at my sides, away from my pockets, so I wouldn't appear a threat. Blair squinted at the rather frayed edges of my black North Face jacket, and their expression morphed from terror to suspicion. "Not child services?" they asked.

Lachlan let go of Blair and hunkered down in front of them. "I promised I wouldn't. Not without your permission."

Blair nodded. "Okay then."

"Matthew's helping me figure out who's been vandalizing my boat. That's all."

Blair's muddy brown eyes blinked rapidly behind their crooked black-rimmed glasses. *A tell.* I'd learned that much from my time at Quest.

"Are you the one who saw the first incident?" I asked gently.

Lachlan shot me a warning glance, but when Blair gulped and nodded, he relaxed. Marginally. "I didn't give anyone your name, Blair, so you don't need to say anything if you don't want to. We can handle this without getting you involved."

"N-no. I want to. I saw the first time." They twisted their fingers together, hampered by the oversized gray sweater that hung past the ragged edges of their jacket sleeves and extended past their knuckles. "But not this time."

Lachlan stood slowly. "This time?"

Blair nodded again, not meeting Lachlan's gaze. "I heard them running, but didn't see anything but their back." They pointed down the dock. "Over there."

"Did you see their car?"

Blair shook their head. "It wasn't in the lot. They ducked into the alley next to the bait and tackle shop. Their car must have been on Front Street, because I heard somebody drive away."

Lachlan muttered a soft curse, but when Blair seemed to shrink into the collar of their jacket, he patted the kid on the shoulder. "Not mad at you, jo. Just wondering what devilment is on deck now."

I tried to arrange my face into its most unthreatening expression. "Blair, can you tell us what time you saw this person?"

With another nervous glance at Lachlan, who was now staring at his boat as if he could discover any problem with the force of his mind, Blair said, "It was right after Lachlan drove away this morning. Around seven?"

Lachlan stopped trying to X-ray his boat with his glare. He lifted an eyebrow and looked down at Blair. "I'm not going to ask you what you were doing on the dock at seven."

Blair dropped their gaze and scuffed one battered high top along the pavement. "I was on my way to the school bus."

"Last I checked, the bus was the other direction and you don't catch it until eight." Blair's mouth firmed into a mulish line but they didn't reply or even look up. Lachlan sighed. "Never mind."

I pulled a business card out of my pocket and held it out. "Blair, if you think of anything else, or if the person comes back, or if you need anything and Lachlan's not around, please give me a call. Okay?"

At first, I didn't think Blair would take the card, but then they plucked it out of my fingers and stowed it in their jacket pocket.

"Did you need anything, jo?" Blair shook their head, and Lachlan jerked his chin at me. "Guess we'd better survey the damage, eh?"

"Ah. Right. I'll...get my camera." I trotted back to the truck and retrieved my bag, taking my time to shut my door and Lachlan's as well so he'd have a chance to speak with Blair without me eavesdropping. I didn't think of myself as particularly intimidating, but the kid was clearly skittish around me. I tried not to take it as an insult. They probably just didn't want to discuss anything personal in front of a stranger.

By the time I rejoined Lachlan on the dock, Blair was gone.

"So, the kid," I said as I hurried to keep up with Lachlan's long-legged stride. "You called them Jo. I thought their name was Blair?"

Lachlan gave me a sharp glance. "How'd you know what pronouns to use for them?"

I shrugged. "I didn't want to make assumptions."

"Jo's just a Scottish endearment. Means dear."

"Are they homeless?"

Lachlan sighed again as he led me toward the boat. "They'd be better off if they were homeless. At least then I could get them some help. But they've got a father, more's the pity. He does just enough to keep child services from taking charge of Blair and has managed to put enough fear into the poor mite that they go along with the lie."

We reached the short gangway that led to the boat's rear deck. Before Lachlan could grab the railing, I put a hand on his arm. "Wait."

He glanced from my hand to my face, and I let go. "Why? Whatever's in there has had most of the day to stew. The sooner I get it out, the better."

I gave him a glare of my own. "It's a fresh crime scene. Or it could be. This is our chance to examine it *before* you clear away all the evidence." I nodded at the railing. "Or contaminate it with your own fingerprints."

He huffed, as if he wanted to disagree, but stepped back. "Wyn isn't stupid. He'd have worn gloves or wiped everything down. Besides, he's been on the boat before, so it's not as though his fingerprints won't be everywhere."

Believe it or not, I can be moderately professional and diplomatic when necessary. Lachlan was the client, so if only to preserve my employment, I needed to cut him some slack—or at least not piss him off any further. I attempted a placating smile. "I get that. But it never hurts to be thorough, and courts— even the supe tribunal—are very fond of evidence. So maybe let me do my job? That's why you hired Quest in the first place, right?"

Lachlan didn't look at me, his gaze fixed on the horizon and the muscles tight in his jaw. But eventually he nodded and let me get to work.

# CHAPTER SEVEN

As I dusted the railing for prints—getting the square root of nothing for my trouble—I asked, "So Blair saw Wyn toss the first fish? Why not use their testimony then?"

"It wouldn't do any good."

"Because they're human and can't testify before a supe tribunal?"

Lachlan glared at me from where he was perched on a weathered wooden bollard. "I don't want this to go to a tribunal."

I looked up from my latest failure to lift a latent print. "You don't? Then why hire us?"

He carded his fingers through his hair, causing it to fall in those very distracting Jason Momoa waves. "I don't want Wyn to suffer. I don't want him punished. I just want him to stop. Besides, Blair couldn't identify Wyn even if I were willing to expose them to the danger of any supernatural shite."

"Why not? Did they only see the first perp from the back too?"

"Oh no. They saw him full frontal for at least ten minutes while Wyn scared up the bollocks to toss the poor herring. But Blair's got prosopagnosia."

"They've got what now?"

"Prosopagnosia. Facial blindness. They can't recognize faces."

I blinked. "At all?"

Lachlan shrugged. "Not as a whole. Unless someone has a really unusual feature, they can't differentiate one face from another." He shrugged again. "And when you think about it, most people aren't all that different. Eyes. Nose. Mouth." He waved a hand at himself. "It's easy for Blair to recognize me because of my size and my hair. Wyn's pretty average size. Nice looking." He snorted. "Pretty, when it comes to that, but his features are very regular."

"Good to know," I grumbled as I bundled my fingerprint kit into its spot in my bag. "Then how do you know Wyn flung the first fish?"

He smiled wryly, which added a trace of vulnerability to his face that...*damn, just damn.* "Wyn may not be stupid, but he's got his blind spots. He was wearing his favorite coat—a red suede designer number with an asymmetric zipper. Blair might not recognize faces, but they can spot things that stick out, and that coat on this dock was a dead giveaway."

I climbed up the port stairs and glanced around the deck. "Do you see anything out of place up here?"

Lachlan mounted the starboard flight, squinting around at the controls, and shook his head. He'd already checked the storage locker where Dead Herring #2 had shown up. "Guess we'd better go below. You first." He gestured for me to precede him. "It's your show and all."

"Right. Thanks." I took it slow as I quartered the deck, photographing every inch, although everything looked as pristine as if an entire fleet of brownies had just departed with their buckets and mops.

Once we got below, though, Lachlan froze, his gaze riveted on the stern. "My cabin. I didn't dog that hatch." He lunged past me.

"Lachlan, wait."

He didn't, of course. He unlatched the pocket door, slid it aside, aaaaannnd...

*Whew!*

Neither one of us had to wonder about what the mysterious visitor had been up to now because the dead-fish stench rolled out in an almost visible wave, along with a blast of very unseasonal heat. The blanket on the oversized bunk sported a decidedly herring-shaped lump in its center.

Lachlan cursed, long and low. He snaked one long arm into the cabin and I heard something click. "It wasn't enough to violate my bed. Did he have to turn on the space heater too?"

"Could I..."

He stood aside as much as possible given the size of his shoulders and chest. "Do your worst. But it's pretty obvious, isn't it? He doesn't want to be married to me anymore, but I didn't think he hated me this much."

"The sundering's going forward, isn't it? Despite the... complications?"

He nodded. "I called to let him know that he could name the date." His wry smile didn't reach his eyes. "He's not taking my calls."

"Maybe the message went astray then. Maybe this is just a—" The incoming call beep from my cell phone interrupted me. I scrabbled it out of my pocket and saw Mal's name on the screen. "Mal? Did you meet with Wyn?"

"No." Mal's tone was equal parts disgusted and apologetic. "He wasn't at his place. Well, his and Lachlan's. Apparently he's moved in with his new bloke."

I glanced at Lachlan. "Uh... You mean...?"

"Aye. He's camped out, snug as you please, at the Martinson estate."

For some reason, the idea of Wyn cozied up in a West Hills mansion while Lachlan made do with the cramped quarters on his boat, not to mention sharing said cramped quarters with random dead fish, really ticked me off. I backed away from where he was staring at that telltale lump, his fists flexing at his sides.

"Are you going over there to question him?" I said, keeping my voice low.

For a moment, Mal didn't respond, which was weird. Mal *always* had a comeback. Working with him and Niall was like sitting center court at Wimbledon, if Wimbledon contended snark instead of tennis. "Thing is, mate, I've got to head into Faerie. Niall too."

"What for?"

"Unknown. Their newlywed majesties have asked for a word, and while I'm pleased to ignore the Queen as much as I'm able, Niall has a certain affection for his brother." Mal chuckled softly. "I've got a soft spot for the big blighter myself, but the summons is a tad awkward."

I sighed. "Yeah. Especially since our fish flinger just struck again."

"Grand," Mal muttered. "Well, I suppose it can't be Wyn, then, considering he's a good hour or more from the coast."

"Not the best alibi, since the flinging occurred around seven this morning. He could have gotten back to Portland in plenty of time." A sort of inverse of Lachlan's trajectory. Hell, they could have passed on the highway. Although... "Any idea if an FTA driver made a drop off at the Martinson estate this morning?"

"Who knows? Niall's kingly brother is a stickler for client confidentiality, but since we're answering his call, maybe I can put in request for a little quid pro quo and get him to pull the logs."

"Good."

"Listen, mate. I don't think we should dawdle overlong on Lachlan's case. I'd like to get it sewn up before their majesties drop something dire on our heads. Could you head over to the Martinson place and interview Wyn?"

I fumbled my phone, barely catching it before it could tumble to the deck. "You want me to handle an interrogation? Without you or Niall?"

Mal chuckled again. "Let's not call it an interrogation. No bright lights and bad coffee needed. Just ask a few questions. If the whole thing is the result of relationship drama, then it might be simple enough to get the bloke to say *Sorry, won't happen again.*"

I thought of Lachlan's violated bed, and the bookings he said he'd lost. As a former freelance photographer, I was well aware that when you were self-employed, the only job you could count on was yesterday's. "What about compensatory damages?"

"Eh, shite." He sighed. "Maybe leave that on the table. We'll get our pet advocate on the line to figure something out."

*Our pet advocate.* Mal and his jokes. The only advocate we contracted with was Quentin Bertrand-Harrington, incubus.

Ted's husband.

"Right," I croaked.

"One other thing, boyo. Keep Lachlan far away from the place. Don't tell him where Wyn is and for the Goddess's sake, don't bring him with you. He'll do something to incriminate himself and suddenly he'll be paying Wyn for the privilege of tossing chum all over his boat."

"I'll try." Although considering Lachlan's size and that I was human and he wasn't, the best I could hope for was misdirection until I could get back to Ted's cave above Dewton and call my FTA driver.

"You'll be brilliant."

I blinked and held the phone away from my ear for a moment to make sure I wasn't hallucinating. "I will?"

"Hugh. *Matt.*" Mal's voice gentled on my real name. "You're a good bloke. You do a good job. Niall and me...well, we're lucky to have you on our team."

I swallowed hard. "You are?"

"Couldn't do without you." A voice rumbled in the background. "I've got to go. I'll keep Zeke in the loop about our progress. But you've got this, mate. We've got faith." He hung up.

I took a moment to stop hyperventilating, then tucked my phone in my pocket. *They've got faith.* I glanced at the vast expanse of Lachlan's back. *I'm not sure I do.* He hadn't punched a wall or anything, which probably had more to do with not wanting to damage his boat than any kind of self-restraint. But the guy was enormous. How was I supposed to keep him away from the upcoming "interview" if he decided he wanted to be there?

*Get over yourself, Steinitz.* I squared my shoulders and marched the two steps it took to reach him. "I know you probably want to get the bed cleaned up, but I should really document the scene beforehand. Then I can get out of your hair." Lachlan didn't respond, other than to curl his enormous hands into fists the size of hams. "Lachlan?"

He whirled, and I stumbled back a step. My face must have given away my fear because his crumpled. "Ah, shite. Sorry. I didn't mean to…" He covered his face with both hands, his big shoulders rising with an enormous breath. Jeez, he must have three times my lung capacity. Then he dropped his hands and gave me a look that was almost apologetic. "I can't… Will you be all right here to do your"—he gestured toward the berth—"whatever you need to do? I've got to"—another gesture, this time in the vague direction of the ocean.

"Oh. Right." I flattened myself against the wall, and a smile tugged at his grim mouth.

"That won't fly, lad. Duck into the head there, if you wouldn't mind."

I got out of his way and he snagged his pack off the compact dining table and surged up onto the deck.

Sue me, okay? I couldn't resist creeping up and peering through the hatch to see what he was doing. And what he was doing, you ask?

Well, besides extracting a bulky folded *something* out of the pack, he was stripping. All the way down. Should I have ducked below again and gotten on with my job? Yes. And before you think I only wanted to ogle his ass and…other things, that's not the reason. In fact, I kept my eyes focused firmly above his waist.

Really. I'm not kidding. Because if you haven't picked up the two major things about me, here they are. One: My heart belongs to Ted Farnsworth, even though he doesn't want it. And two: I am utterly captivated by anything or anybody supernatural.

So what I wanted at that moment was to see what a selkie did to comfort himself when his life was imploding. An invasion of privacy? Yes. But I needed to understand Lachlan if I was going to help him, and his selkie nature was a big part of that understanding.

Once he was naked—no, I *didn't* look!—Lachlan shook out the bundle. When you hear about a selkie shedding his skin, it sounds kind of creepy, right? Like, well, the skin should look like a seal with its insides scooped out, maybe with empty eyes and sagging jaw and flopping flippers and now I'm creeping *myself* out. But it wasn't like that at all.

It was almost like Lachlan was donning a wetsuit, albeit one covered in a layer of short, glossy brown fur. And no, it didn't have a merman-ish tail. Two legs, two arms, just like an ordinary wetsuit, and the hood that hung down his back as he made his way to the stern didn't look like a creepy seal mask at all.

He slipped over the side with not even a splash. I hurried up the stairs and over to the rail in time to see a seal—a really *big* seal—head out into the bay.

"Well," I muttered, "that takes care of keeping him away from the interview."

Which was why I felt comfortable staying on deck and watching until the seal finally dove out of sight under the waves.

# CHAPTER EIGHT

Lachlan hadn't returned by the time I'd photographed every square inch of the boat, including the—ewww!—extremely dead fish in the middle of what looked to be a very comfortable berth. Bagging the herring as evidence wasn't the pleasantest task, but I managed. However, I wasn't about to take it with me to my first solo interrogation. Okay, *interview*, but you know what I mean. I dropped it off with Zeke at the Quest offices. *After* I took a shower at my place outside Dewton—it wasn't more than a mile from the bay—and called my FTA driver. Jeez, I'm not a *total* slob.

I took a plain old Uber to the Martinson place, since its West Hills locations wasn't far from the Quest offices in the Pearl district and I didn't know the layout. The FTA can go almost anywhere using Faerie as a shortcut, but the entrance and exit points need to be hidden from random human view. The Uber driver whistled as she dropped me at the wrought-iron gates.

"Fancy friends you've got. Must be nice."

"They're not my friends," I muttered, but boosted her tip in the app, anyway. Then I stood there like one of those turned-to-stone trolls Mal told me about, because this place was totally outside of anything in my experience—and I traipsed through Faerie on the regular.

I mentioned the gates, right? Curlicues and leaves and a giant stylized M on each section. There was a security keypad to one side, along with an intercom and a security camera, but the gates weren't closed at the moment, so I avoided them. The driveway wasn't long. This was the West Hills, after all. Go too far back and you'd fall off into southwest Portland. But the house looming inside its surrounding stone fence gave the impression that it *deserved* a long driveway, if you know what I mean.

"'Last night I dreamed I went to Manderley again,'" I quoted as I walked along the slate flagstones that led to the door. The lawn was pretty wide by West Hills standards, the landscaping pristine, probably because three gardeners were hustling around with trimmers and rakes and spades. The big white panel truck with the landscapers' plant-themed logo on the side was probably why the gates were open.

One of the gardeners was dead-heading a rose bush in the bed next to the big oak double doors. He smiled sheepishly at me and waggled his fingers. I blinked, nonplussed. Why would a gardener acknowledge me? Then I recognized him. *Ronnie Purl.*

"Ronnie? What are you—" I smacked my forehead. "I mean, obviously you're working for the landscaper, but I thought you were working on Devin's crew."

He shrugged. "Got to do my community service, don't I?" He wrinkled his nose, and with his narrow face and pointed chin, he looked more ferrety than ever. He shrugged one shoulder and snipped another faded rose. "But it's not forever, right?"

"Right. Well." I gave him what I hoped was a reassuring smile. "Keep up the good work."

I mentally rolled my eyes as I rang the bell. *Keep up the good work*? Jeez. Ronnie was probably rolling his eyes for real. Nothing like a little condescension from the *human* to really make his day.

The bell echoed inside as if the house was nothing more than an empty shell, but when the uniformed maid opened the door, it was immediately obvious that wasn't the case. The place was *packed* with stuff: knickknacks on shelves and tables, art and—ugh—trophies on the walls, chinoiserie vases that came up to my waist, and at least two grandfather clocks. And that was just in the entryway.

"May I help you?" the maid asked, which was a perfectly reasonable question and made me stop gaping at what I could see of the house.

"Yeah, um..." I fumbled to get my Quest credentials out of my pocket. Why hadn't I done that before I knocked on the door instead of giving Ronnie Purl a completely unnecessary and probably unwelcome virtual pat on the head? I held out the badge. "I'm Matthew Stein— That is, I'm Hugh from Quest Investigations. I'd like to have a few words with Wyn Ellis, if I may."

To her credit, she didn't blink. "I'm afraid I don't—"

"That's all right, Eleri," a voice boomed from an open door next to one of the clocks. "I'll handle this."

"Of course, Mr. Martinson." Eleri didn't curtsey, but I suspect it was a near thing. Heck, I almost curtsied, because that voice had *authority* to it.

The man who paced into the foyer—tall, lean, and silver-haired—clearly wasn't Wyn's *new bloke*, since by all accounts, Reid might just as well be human. This guy...wasn't that. Nope. Not a chance. This had to be his father. As an elemental magician, Pierce Martinson wielded power on a whole different level than I was used to even though I worked with fae, demons, and shifters. He wore that power as if it were as well-fitting and tailored as his three-piece charcoal suit.

Pierce smoothed his scarlet tie and gestured toward the room he'd just exited. "If you would join me in my study?"

I nodded and shuffled across the polished wood floor. And before you think I was just being subservient, no. The floor was made of three different kinds of wood. I guessed the medium brown main planks were oak, every third one edged with a thinner strip of darker wood. Maybe walnut? But it was the lighter wood, the color of my high school gym floor, that got to me, because it was inlaid in a diagonal pattern that offset the oak and walnut, making it look like waves lapping on the shore. By the time I made it out of the entryway and into the study, I was almost seasick.

To keep from feeling like I was about to get swept away by hardwood undertow, I lifted my gaze to the walls, then wished I hadn't.

"Nice, uh, harpoon," I croaked.

Seriously, this place could give the Herman Melville room at the Sylvia Beach Hotel a run for its money. Although with the marlin above the fireplace, maybe he was going more for an Ernest Hemingway / *Old Man and the Sea* vibe, particularly given the collection of vintage firearms in the glass-fronted case next to the window.

Wait…wasn't this guy supposed to be a *fire* mage? What was with all the water-themed tchotchkes? Could elemental mages master more than one element?

On the other hand, maybe this was his version of a dominance display, proclaiming that fire was more powerful than water by showing all the water-based things he'd conquered.

On the *other* hand—I'd end up with as many hands as a Zeke's demon friend AJ who kept three extra pairs of arms in an alternate dimension at this rate—I knew even less about rich people than I did about elemental mages.

Pierce settled into a red velvet wingback chair next to the fireplace—which, yeah, was roaring away, even though it wasn't all that cold outside. He didn't offer me a seat, not that I'd have taken one anyway since the only available perch was a stool held up with what looked like three alligator legs. And given the pattern of its leather seat, the gator had donated more than its feet to the Martinson's decor.

"Now then," he said, in that deep, cultured voice that befit a tenured professor of philosophy rather than a dude who dabbled in one of the most dangerous magical disciplines. "To what do I owe the honor of your visit?"

"I'm from Quest Investigations." I held out my credentials again, but he waved them away. "We're representing Lachlan Brodie on a matter of some, er, oceanic harassment and would like to speak to his husband. We understand he's staying with you."

Pierce's bland expression didn't change. "Please refer to Mr. Ellis by name rather than as though he were a possession of Mr. Brodie's. Such courtesy would be appropriate even were sundering proceedings not already underway."

Heat rushed up my neck and from the way my forehead burned, I probably looked like I'd just spent all day in a Sheol sauna. "My apologies. I was merely attempting to present the context of the case. I meant no disrespect."

Pierce inclined his head. "Accepted. Now, what business do you have with my future son-in-law?"

I blinked. Future son-in-law? Wyn was planning to marry Reid Martinson before his fae divorce was final? Heck, from what Lachlan had said about the timing, the ink wasn't dry on the magical paperwork yet. Had the jerk been cheating on Lachlan even longer than he suspected? "I won't take much of his time. I'd just like to ask him a few questions about his whereabouts on several occasions, if you don't mind."

"He might not mind, but *I* do." The angry bark from the doorway made me whip around. I whacked a wooden figurine with my elbow but managed to catch it before it toppled off the table. Only when I gingerly placed it upright again did I realize it was a rather gruesome depiction of a naked man being consumed head first by a shark—while flames danced around his bare feet.

"Reid, I can handle this." Pierce's voice held an edge of impatience. "You should remain with Wyn. No doubt he would appreciate your company and support."

Reid Martinson didn't resemble his father at all. While Pierce looked like he'd just stepped out of an Edwardian period drama with an otherworldly twist, Reid would be more at home in a Quentin Tarantino flick—or maybe at a tailgate party. He didn't have the air of *extra* that most supes brought to the table one way or other. In fact, he looked more as though he could be related to *me*.

He was about my height, maybe a little broader across the chest. Same medium brown hair and beard. His clothes didn't come off the rack, though, that much I could tell. His French-cuffed button-down had the sheen of silk, and his charcoal trousers hung without a wrinkle to brush the tops of his Italian leather loafers.

In other words, the value of what he was wearing probably exceeded my clothing budget for the year. Okay, let's be real—for the entire decade. But other than that, other than being obviously rich, he could be anybody at the counter at Wanda's Diner. Guess Reid was overcompensating for his magic-null status with attitude as well as conspicuous consumption.

I tried to smile in a professional and non-confrontational manner. "Only a few questions. Then I'll be on my way."

Reid crossed his arms. "No."

Pierce sighed heavily, the quintessential long-suffering parent. "Reid. There's no harm in cooperating. After all"—he smiled benignly—"we have nothing to hide."

I buried a snort. In my experience, people who claimed to have nothing to hide usually had a boatload of crap stuffed into their virtual closet.

"I don't care," Reid said. "We don't need to talk to this...this *human*. He has no right to stick his nose into our affairs."

I cleared my throat and brandished my credentials. "Actually, I do have the right. Duly authorized by the supe council."

He eyed me with obvious disgust. "Not authorized by me." He grabbed the laminated card out of my hand and squinted at it as if he were checking for signs it was counterfeit. A sly smile spread over his face. "Provisional, eh? Wonder what the council would say if they found out you were harassing one of the foremost magicians in the last three centuries?"

Reid's attitude wasn't new. I'd faced it more often than not over my probationary period. But for some reason, he got in my hair, maybe because, according to Mal's intel, he was no more supernatural than I was. I smiled blandly. "You're a magician? I wasn't aware. I'll be sure to update my notes."

He glared at me, but before he could come up with a retort, a soft voice spoke from the doorway.

"It's all right, Reid. I don't mind answering the gentleman's questions."

# CHAPTER NINE

I don't know what I expected from Wyn Ellis since I had no idea what a Corlun Dwr looked like. I'd seen some decidedly... unusual fae. Just last spring, I'd faced a bean-nighe, and if you'd ever seen one you'd never mistake her for anything but supernatural. Blue skin, hair accessories made of bone, a definite medieval fashion sense. Of course, if you'd ever seen one, chances are you'd be dead, since she's a portent of doom. Pro tip: Keep your laundry locked up when a bean-nighe's in the neighborhood, because once she hangs your drawers out to dry, you're toast.

Given my experience with Mal, Niall, Ted and his incubus husband—who's got *wings* sometimes, just saying—and even Lachlan with his magical shifting wetsuit, though, I expected Wyn to be more...strapping, I guess? But instead he was slim and high-cheekboned and long-legged. More like Zeke, although Zeke had an underlying toughness that Wyn, with his waiflike appearance, lacked.

He was wearing narrow gray trousers and a trendy red jacket that I realized must be the one he was wearing when Blair had seen him at the dock. Yep, if I'd seen that, I wouldn't have forgotten it either.

Because there was no denying that the man was gorgeous. Not my type, but definitely gorgeous. No wonder Lachlan wasn't in a hurry to fae-divorce him.

Reid strode over to him and wrapped a brawny arm across his shoulder. "Babe, you shouldn't be down here. You've been through enough."

I immediately put on my sympathetic expression. "I understand it must be tough to be in such....unfamiliar surroundings." I glanced at a few of Pierce's more alarming accouterments. The gator-footed stool and death-by-shark-and-fire carving weren't the worst, and if this guy was a water sprite, the room probably gave him a case of the dreaded jim-jams. "This won't take long, and then I'm sure everything can be settled to everyone's satisfaction."

Reid shot me a dirty look. "You—"

"Reid," Wyn said, his musical voice weary. "Please." He glanced around the room and shuddered. "But not in here." Yep, definitely the jim-jams. Even if Wyn *was* the fish flinger, I hoped for his sake that Reid wasn't planning on insisting they live in the ancestral pile after their wedding. The poor guy would have nightmares every time he walked to the front door.

And speaking of the front door, was somebody attacking it with a battering ram? The sound of something large hitting it boomed through the hallway, rattling the firearm collection in its case and making the stuffed marlin bounce against the wall as if it was still fighting the hook that landed it.

"What the devil?" Reid muttered as Eleri scurried past the study door.

Her muffled greeting was swallowed by the thunder of a voice I knew well, even after a short acquaintance, and from Wyn's flinch, he recognized it too.

"I need to speak to him. I know he's here." Lachlan didn't shout—he didn't need to. The acoustics in the entryway were like an echo chamber and his deep voice was naturally resonant.

Great, just great. I had one job—well, two, although the interview part wasn't going so well either. But with the failure of the second—keeping Lachlan away from Wyn—job one was about to crash and burn in a big way.

"Eleri! Don't let that bastard in," Reid bellowed.

Although I agreed with the intent of that order—and two minutes ago I would have sworn Reid Martinson and I would never agree on anything from romantic partner to hair care products—I had little confidence that the petite maid would be able to keep Lachlan out if he was determined to get in.

But when all of us—Reid, Wyn, Pierce, and me—boiled out of the creepy-ass study and into the creepy-ass entry, the maid was holding her own.

She hadn't exactly taken root in the hallway—that would have damaged the marble tile—but her arms, now covered in bark, had lengthened. Her elongating fingers were sprouting leaves and some wicked looking thorns.

*Dryad.* Figures. Jeez, I couldn't get away from them today.

I spared a moment to wonder how a dryad felt working for a fire mage, but then Lachlan spotted Wyn through the extemporaneous foliage. I expected him to be angry. Furious, even, considering he'd probably need to replace his berth. But instead, he just looked sad. Defeated. *Betrayed.*

"Why, Wyn? You'd no call to—"

"Don't talk to him, you savage bastard," Reid snarled. "Haven't you hurt him enough?"

I blinked, my gaze darting from Lachlan to Wyn, who'd huddled in on himself, looking as though he'd shrunk two inches. Had Lachlan *abused* him? Is that why Wyn felt justified in striking back?

Lachlan ignored Reid and Wyn ignored Lachlan and Pierce ignored everybody, apparently checking his watch against the two grandfather clocks, which had both started chiming the hour.

*Guess it's up to me.* "Wyn, did you place dead fish on Lachlan's boat?"

"Don't answer," Reid snapped. "You don't owe him anything."

Wyn placed a hand on Reid's chest, and Lachlan winced slightly at that sign of trust and affection. "I owe him the truth. He's still my husband."

"He never should have been." Reid shot Lachlan a murderous glance. "You should never have picked him. He doesn't deserve you. He doesn't have money, he looks like he's spent the last decade roaming the woods, and he has the temper of a grizzly."

Actually, the only grizzly I knew was the sweetest guy on the planet—which was probably the reason I was still in love with him. I cleared my throat. "If we could return to the question. Did you place the fish on the boat?"

Wyn dropped his hand from Reid and laced his fingers together. "Yes," he whispered. "But I'm not even sure why I did it. It was just a…an impulse."

"An impulse?" I frowned. "Once is an impulse. Four times is—"

Wyn straightened, his eyes wide. "Four? No, I… Once. Only once."

"So you're saying you only vandalized Mr. Brodie's boat on one occasion?"

He paled, which considering he wasn't exactly rosy beforehand, did him no favors. "Vandalized? I only tossed a fish onto the deck. Lachlan runs fishing cruises. The deck has fish on it all the time."

"So you deny placing additional, er, deceased sea life in the aft locker, on the engine block, and on the berth, thereby causing him financial and emotional harm."

"Oi!" Lachlan said. "Enough with the emotional harm!"

"What?" Wyn whispered. "The… No!"

"There are significant damages on the table," I said softly. "It would be better if we could come to an arrangement privately, don't you think?"

Wyn's eyes widened even further. "I swear I didn't… It was only because of the sundering, and I—"

"Wyn, lad," Lachlan said tiredly, "I never wanted you to be unhappy."

"That's rich," Reid sneered. "You didn't care how he felt. You only cared about your *ego*. You flat out refused. You made him *beg*."

"There was no begging, you wanker," Lachlan growled. "I made a promise and so did he. I wasn't about to break it unless he was sure."

"He was sure. Sure that you're a brutish slacker who—"

"Eleri," Pierce said mildly, "if you wouldn't mind, I believe our guest is leaving."

For a moment, I thought that Pierce was about to toss Wyn out of the house for being a phantom fish flinger. But after Eleri defoliated herself and held the door while gazing pointedly at me, I realized *I* was the guest in question.

Jeez, if I ever expected to be a full-fledged investigator, I needed to manage interviews better than this. However, it was clear that Wyn wouldn't be able to answer anything sensibly while Reid and Lachlan were sniping at each other over his head. I pulled a card out of my breast pocket and held it out to him. "If you think of anything else you'd like to add—"

"He won't." Reid tried to snatch the card out of my hand, but Wyn blocked him neatly with nothing more than a reproachful glance.

"Thank you." Wyn tucked it into the inside pocket of his jacket, his gaze shifting to Lachlan. "I'm sorry too. I never wanted you to do anything you didn't want to. Truly."

I tried to walk out with as much dignity as possible. So of course I tripped on the rug inside the door and fell right into Lachlan's arms as he was stepping over the threshold. By the time he untangled me from his chest and set me on my feet on the porch, the door was shut firmly behind us.

Mindful of the gardeners all peering at us surreptitiously out of the corners of their eyes—all except Ronnie Purl, who was blatantly staring, his jaw slack—I tried to shove Lachlan down the steps and up the drive, which was like trying to push a boulder uphill.

"Jeez, now I know what Sisyphus felt like," I muttered.

"This how Quest handles business, is it? You bolluxed that up royally."

"*I* bolluxed it up?" With one final shove, we made it through the gates, which swung shut behind us. Guess keeping us out was more important than the inconvenience of keeping the gardeners in. "What are you doing here? Mal *told* you that you weren't supposed to be present during the interview!"

Surprisingly, pink bloomed under the brown of Lachlan's cheeks. "That was when Mal was doing the questioning." He dropped his gaze to his feet. "I thought you might need some help, you being...well..."

"Human?" I said dryly.

His chin jerked up. "Unfamiliar with the bloody Martinsons. They're a piece of work, and no mistake."

"So you know them?"

"Unfortunately," he growled.

Something Reid said tickled at the back of my mind. "Inside just now, Reid said Wyn should never have picked you. Did he mean that Wyn should have picked him instead? Was Reid one of his other...suitors?"

"Suitors?" Lachlan's lips quirked. "Been reading historical romance, have you?"

It was my turn to flush. I remembered that Mal had been one of Wyn's sexual partners. "I was trying to be polite."

Lachlan hitched his backpack onto his shoulder. "No need to pull your punches with me. I'm no blushing flower."

I remembered the thorns on the maid's fingers. "I'm beginning to think nobody is."

"To answer your question, Reid was sniffing around Wyn back when we were...courting."

"Courting?" I lifted an eyebrow. "Now who's been boning up on their historical romances?"

He snorted. "Don't have to read 'em, do I? I lived them."

I blinked. "Er...how old are you?"

He lifted an eyebrow—the one with the scar running through it, which gave it an extra quirk. "Old enough."

I sighed. Supe lifespans were something that I still hadn't gotten a good handle on. From what I could tell, some of them could be as close to immortal as made no difference. "Look, Wyn admitted to the first incident, which was annoying but not damaging, right?"

"Other than to my self-esteem," he replied.

"Well, we've already established that you're no blushing flower, so that makes your self-esteem immaterial. Do you believe him when he says he wasn't responsible for the others?"

Lachlan stared meditatively through the iron gates. "I...don't know. I'd like to say he never lied to me, but isn't promising to be true and then shagging another man a lie? He didn't hide it, but..." He shrugged. "If he wasn't guilty, though, why hide out with the Martinsons?"

I bit my lip. This wasn't going to be an easy question. "Did you ever... I mean, would Wyn have any reason to believe that you mean him bodily harm?"

Lachlan glared at me, his face a mask of absolute fury. "You're asking if I beat my husband? Goddess bless, what kind of man do you think I am?"

It was my turn to shrug. "The kind I don't know very well?"

He hitched his backpack onto his shoulder again. "No," he said through bared teeth. "I never did." He turned on his heel and strode off down the street.

"Wait!" I called, running to keep up. "Where are you going?"

"To call one of your bloody FTA drivers so I can get home and find out if I've got another load of offal piled on my boat." He lengthened his stride. "Don't call me," he said as he increased the distance between us. "I'll call you."

"Right," I muttered as he disappeared into a copse of Doug fir. "I'll expect that right around the time pigs start dive-bombing my Honda."

# CHAPTER
## TEN

But as it happened, Lachlan called me long before the end of the world. Barely six hours later, as a matter of fact. I was still at the Quest office, even though Zeke had long since left. His drummer boyfriend—who's a kangaroo shifter, by the way—had a concert, and Zeke never missed them if he could manage it.

I was trying to figure out the best way to wrangle my report on Lachlan's case without explicitly saying *I screwed it up*. So when my cell phone rang, I didn't even check the screen for the caller ID. In fact, I had my eyes clenched shut because I expected it to be Mal wanting an update, and I was hoping that the inside of my eyelids might suddenly flash an explanation that didn't make me look like a total idiot.

"H'lo," I said glumly.

"Is this Matthew?"

The way the caller pronounced my name—*MattHugh*—would have given him away even if his voice hadn't already been imprinted in my brain. "Lachlan?" I huffed and leaned back in my chair. "This is a surprise."

"Trust me, lad, you're not nearly as surprised as I am," he muttered, which wasn't exactly complimentary, but hey, in his place I wouldn't be waxing effusive either. "I...need your help."

I sat up, my nerves pinging with a little adrenaline rush. Can you blame me? If a supe asked *you* for help—assuming it wasn't a vampire in search of a midnight snack, a necromancer shopping for life essence to power a curse, or, you know, a feral dryad—wouldn't you jump at the chance? "What's up?"

"I'm at St. Stupid's."

"The hospital?" The supe community referred to the paranormal wing of United Memorial Hospital as St. Stupid's for some reason. "Are you all right?"

"Got a lump on my head the size of a duck egg with a headache to match, but that's not the biggest problem. I'd rather not discuss it over the phone though, and since I'm checking out AWA—"

"A-W what now?"

"Against witch advice. The bloody doctor keeps going on about natural consequences and won't let me go without an escort."

I frowned as I scrabbled my notes into Lachlan's case file. "Did they treat you for a concussion?" As far as I knew, the medimagical staff at St. Stupid's—from their witch paramedics to the demon diagnostician to the *achubyddion* healers who tapped into the very essence of a supernatural being—could handle about anything.

"They tried. I refused."

"For goodness sake, why?"

Lachlan mumbled something. I thought I picked out the word *deserve* in there. Was the big idiot refusing treatment to punish himself?

I shoved the file into my desk drawer and locked it, and then tried to shrug into my jacket while keeping my phone pressed to my ear. "I'll come, but don't be foolhardy. Let them treat you. Because if there's something really wrong, something other than medically—"

"There is."

I grabbed my bag and hoofed it up the stairs to the fourth floor portal. "Then you need to be 100% to face it. You've got time. But I'm not going anywhere with you until you're cleared by the doctor."

"I need to get out—"

"Stay. Put." I reached the fourth floor corridor. "Please."

"Then get your sweet arse over here now."

He cut the connection before I could pick my jaw off the floor. *Sweet arse?* He thought my ass was sweet? Nah. It was probably just something he said to anybody whenever they got in his hair.

I strode over to the door next to the twin vending machines. It didn't look any different than all the other doors in the office, but this one couldn't be more unusual. Punch in the right code on the keypad next to it and you could end up in Faerie. Or—because a lot of our cases involved finding people whose health could be compromised—in a special room next to the St. Stupid's ER.

I keyed in that code and stepped through into the dim, green-walled space. It had extra high ceilings since some supes were on the tall side, and held no furniture since they needed room for a gurney, not to mention random wings, horns, extraneous limbs, and general flailing.

Luckily, it was empty at the moment. A duergar with a broken finger had nearly taken my head off once. I mean, seriously? Those guys drink fermented dragon bile infused with crushed holly berries but they're total babies when it comes to injuries. Maybe because they're not injured all that often—their bones are practically made of stone and their skin is like leather.

I slipped out the door, but then stood there like a dolt. Lachlan had so thrown me off with his remark—totally not specific!—about my ass that I hadn't gotten his room number.

"Crap," I muttered.

"Hugh? What are you doing here?"

I turned at the sound of Jordan's voice. The young were was standing next to the nurse's station in his Wonderful Mug apron, one hand sporting a wide gauze bandage. "I could ask you the same, but I can guess. Another run in with the milk steamer?"

Jordan colored. "Maybe." He glanced sulkily at the nurse. "My hand is fine. I don't know why I need the bandage."

The nurse gave him a stern look. "Because you work with humans, Jordan. Secrecy Pact, remember? They expect you to have a burn to recover from."

"Whatever," he muttered.

I sidled up to the counter. "Good evening. I'm here to see Lachlan Brodie. He's expecting me."

The nurse blinked at me. "Um…" She wasn't someone I'd met before, so she was probably weighing her options about finding a human in the supe-only ER.

Jordan clapped me on the back. "Don't worry, Renee. Hugh works with Quest Investigations. He's totally legit." He nudged me with his elbow. "Go ahead. Show her your badge." Jordan's expression turned wistful as I pulled my credentials out. "Wish I had a badge."

Renee returned my credentials along with a lime green visitor badge, which clearly wasn't the kind Jordan was mooning over. I doubted he needed one of these—he was so accident prone he was practically a St. Stupid's resident. "Mr. Brodie is on the third floor, diagnostic wing. Do you know the way?"

"I've never been but—"

"Oh! I can show him!" Jordan said.

"I think I can probably find my way, Jordan, but thanks."

He grinned sunnily. "No, see, that's the thing. You're human, so the hospital spells'll probably redirect you and dump you out on the human side of the building, even with the visitor's badge. But if I'm with you, you won't have a problem."

I raised my eyebrows at Renee. "Is that true?"

She shrugged. "He's not entirely wrong. We're not really set up to allow humans in here unescorted. The badge will keep people from trying to kick you out, but if Jordan is willing to take you up, I won't have to call an orderly. Since we're a little busy today..."

I shook my head, laughing at the way Jordan was almost vibrating with excitement. "In that case, thanks, Jordan. Lead the way."

He grabbed my arm and tugged me toward a bank of elevators. "Have you ever been to the diagnostic wing? Oh wait, you said you hadn't." He poked the elevator call button, wrinkling his nose. "I have. When that epidemic hit last summer and I was one of the only werewolves who didn't get sick, I practically *lived* up there while they ran about a billion tests on me to try to figure out why." When the car arrived, we stepped inside and Jordan punched the button for the third floor. "Of course, I also had a broken leg and a bunch of other stuff so I guess it was easier for them to keep me there instead of making one of the orderlies wheel me up and down all the time."

The arrival alert dinged and the doors slid open. We headed out of the elevator lobby and past the nurse's station. But when we rounded the desk, I stumbled back with a gasp, banging my hip on a rolling metal cart and sending it careening away in a rattle of bedpans. The hallway was blocked by a large pair of all too familiar leathery black wings. The first time I'd seen those wings was when Quentin Bertrand-Harrington caught me making a pass at Ted.

Incubi have wings. I think I mentioned that, right? Really, really big ones. Since I didn't know incubi existed back then, they, er, made an impression. In fact, Quentin's wings—not to mention his claws—were the first up-close-and-personal proof I had that the supernatural truly existed.

But let's be real, okay? No matter how I felt about Ted, I would never have made a move on him if I'd known he was married at the time. He told me his wedding was off—but it was off because he'd somehow gotten married to Quentin instead of Rusty Johnson, his original fiancé.

Even though my relationship with Quentin was okay now—more or less—it was never good when his wings made an appearance. Usually, it meant that Ted was in danger.

"Hugh?" Jordan's tone was laced with confusion as he captured the cart and placed it back against the wall . "Are you okay?" He glanced over his shoulder. "Oh, you don't need to worry about AJ. He's cool. Same as Zeke." Jordan screwed up his face. "Although usually he doesn't let his wings out in the corridors. Too many things to knock over."

AJ? Oh, right. The demon diagnostic technician, *not* Quentin. Incubi weren't the only supes with wings. Sometimes I forgot that little detail. I took a deep, settling breath and smiled tightly at Jordan. "I've heard of him, but I've never met him."

"He's really nice. So's his boyfriend. Look! He's here too. Hi, Wash!"

A man with nearly black hair and warm brown skin peered over the edge of AJ's wing, worry infusing his handsome face.

"Jordan," I murmured, "maybe we shouldn't intrude. They're probably busy. If you could show me to Lachlan's room, I'll just slip inside and get out of everyone's way."

"That might be a little tough. They're standing right in front of it." He winced. "With Dr. Mori. She's scary." He leaned closer and whispered out of the side of his mouth. "Kitsune. You don't mess with them."

Dr. Mori must be the slender woman with the smooth cap of dark hair. Sure enough, several fox tails were swishing under the hem of her white lab coat. Jordan took my elbow and led me toward the group. Considering his usual exuberance was significantly toned down, I wasn't sure whether he was holding on to me for my benefit or his.

"Wash, AJ, Dr. Mori. This is Hugh, from Quest Investigations. He's here for Lachlan…" Jordan's nose twitched, and he turned a little green. "Ugh. Do I smell *fish*?"

Dr. Mori turned her severe gaze on Jordan. "Mr. Tate. Please limit your remarks to what is absolutely necessary."

"Matthew!" Lachlan roared from inside the room. "For the love of the Goddess, get in here."

Wash lifted a sardonic eyebrow. "I take it you're who he's been waiting for."

"He called me to meet him here, yes."

"In that case," Dr. Mori said, zero nonsense in her tone, "you can turn around and leave. Mr. Brodie will not be exiting this hospital until I clear him medically." She shot a glare through the open door. "Which will not be until one of our *achubydd* consultants treats his head injury."

"Head injury?" Alarm zinged down my spine. "Is he okay?"

"He will be. Provided he follows my orders. Otherwise, his injury will not be his only problem." She gave a curt nod to Wash and AJ. "I'll be in my office. Inform me when the *achubydd* arrives."

# CHAPTER
## ELEVEN

Wash had been rubbing AJ's arms soothingly this whole time, and the demon's wings were now folded even if they weren't fully retracted. "It's okay, babe."

"It's not," AJ said miserably.

Wash glanced at Jordan and me. "We should let Hugh in to see Lachlan. You've done all you can and we can wait for Ewan just as well by the elevator as here. Okay?" AJ nodded and allowed Wash to lead him away.

Jordan stared quizzically after them. "What do you suppose that was about?"

I pointed a finger at the center of his chest. "Whatever it is, you're to keep your nose out of it. Sometimes I'd swear you were a cat shifter, not a werewolf at all."

Jordan gave me a disgusted look. "You don't have to be insulting." His nose twitched again. "*Fish.* Why does it have to be fish?" He started to walk into the room, but I stopped him with a hand on his arm.

"Jordan. I'm grateful for your escort, but this is a Quest case. You can go now."

He blinked his big brown eyes. "But—" He sighed, shoulders slumping. "Fine. I'll wait out here though. You'll need me to walk you out."

I suspected I could find my own way well enough, but when Lachlan bellowed my name again, I decided to let it be. I knew from experience that talking Jordan around wasn't the work of a minute. Or even ten. I slipped into the room and approached the bed.

"Hey." I studied Lachlan's face. His usual scowl was in place, but his tanned skin had a grayish cast. He obviously wasn't up to walking out of here, even without Dr. Mori's ultimatum. "What happened? You look like crap."

He cut me an irritated glare. "I'm aware." He ran a hand through his hair, and when he winced, I noticed that an area under his ear was shaved. "I was mugged."

"Mugged?" I goggled at him. "What boneheaded mugger would attack *you*? You're as big as a Humvee."

His lips twitched. "Even a Humvee can get T-boned if the driver isn't paying attention."

"Were you? T-boned, I mean? Is your truck okay?" I frowned. "Wait a minute. You don't have your truck."

He gave me another patented Lachlan Brodie glare. "That's right. I took your bloody FTA, didn't I? And look where it got me."

"You were mugged in *Faerie*?" Holy crap, the King was going to have a fit.

"No. I was in that stand of trees at the end of the road, digging around for the return token, when I got coshed."

"Did you see who it was?"

"I was too busy being unconscious, thanks." He winced again. "Paramedics said I'd been out for at least thirty minutes, although I can't remember it. Not even sure how anybody found me to call 9-1-1, but whoever it was had to be a supe, since I ended up with the St. Stupid's SMTs."

SMTs. Supernatural Medical Technicians. Most of them were witches, so if they said Lachlan had been out for half an hour, they were probably accurate down to the second. "It sounds like they're expecting an *achubydd* to come round to treat you, and from what I've heard, that's pretty much instant. So you shouldn't be stuck here much longer."

He grabbed my hand, his grip surprisingly gentle. "That won't help. Not entirely." He swallowed convulsively. "The mugger took my pack."

"Oookay. Is there—"

"My pack with *my seal skin* inside."

My eyes widened. Without his skin, he couldn't shift. And if somebody knew that, if they knew what the skin was for, they could control Lachlan's life. "Oh."

His grip tightened. "I have to get it back, Matthew. If I don't, I'll never be well again. Never *whole* again. You need to help me get out of here so I can find it." He let go of me and took hold of his IV line, but I grabbed his wrist.

"No. You stay here. Wait for the *achubydd*. At least get your *physical* injuries repaired. I'll find the pack."

His skeptical expression didn't do much for my self-esteem. "You? How will you manage that?"

"I work for an investigation company, remember? This is what we do." Not that I'd ever done it on my own before, but if I couldn't handle it, I'd swallow my pride and call Mal or Niall. I gave his wrist a little shake. "Stay here. Let them treat you. Promise?"

He narrowed his eyes, because he knew that *I* knew that if he made a promise, he'd keep it. He sighed, and he must really have felt horrible because he didn't fight any more. "All right. I promise."

"Good. I'll keep you posted." I let go of his arm and pointed at his face. "But no more showing up at places unannounced. Get it?"

He nodded curtly. "Got it."

"Good." I strode for the door.

"Matthew?"

I turned at the uncertainty in his tone. "Yes?"

He smiled, slow and so sweet he could almost be Ted. I felt that smile low in my belly. "Thank you."

I scuttled out of the room before I could do anything stupid like fall for another unavailable supe. Since I was aiming for speed rather than accuracy, I ran full tilt into Jordan, who was still lurking right outside the door.

"*Oof.*" He rubbed his chest. "Sorry."

"Don't be. I was the one who ran into you." I edged past him. "But if you don't mind, I need to hurry."

"I don't mind." He grinned at me, bouncing on his toes. "Where are we going?"

"*We* are not going anywhere. *I* am going to track down a missing—" I clamped my lips together. *Client privilege.*

"A missing pack. I heard."

I rolled my eyes. "Jordan. Seriously?"

He gave me the patented werewolf puppy eyes. "Come on, Hugh. I may be lousy with the milk steamer"—he brandished his unnecessary bandage—"but I'm *super* good at finding things."

I hesitated. I didn't really want to bring Jordan in on a case, at least not purposely. We had enough problems when he inserted himself accidentally. On the other hand, what experience did *I* have in locating missing articles, since apparently when it came to falling for the wrong guy, I couldn't find my common sense with both hands and a GPS?

"Are you sure you could track it?"

Jordan wrinkled his nose again. "If he was carrying it, then yeah. Smells kind of…rub off. And fish is one thing that I *never* mistake." He grinned. "Mostly so I can avoid it."

I glanced back at the door and lowered my voice. "He's not a fish. He's a selkie. A seal shifter."

"I get that. There's the whole ocean vibe. But he's been *near* a fish lately." His nostrils flared. "For that matter, so have you."

"Hey!" I said indignantly. "I cleaned up afterward."

"Like I said, smells rub off. And linger." He patted my arm. "But don't worry. Not for*ever.*"

"Right. Let's go."

I didn't want to take the FTA back to the place where Lachlan was attacked. For one thing, the scene had already been contaminated by the SMTs. The supe community didn't have a law enforcement branch per se—they dispensed justice through their councils. If they received a complaint, they could haul in the suspected perp and subject them to the same truth spell that had gotten me to declare my enduring love for Ted in front of— among others—Ted's husband, not to mention the Queen of Faerie, the high druid elder, and the dragon shifter queen. That's why they needed Quest in the first place. They wanted investigations carried out by their own, discreetly.

I had to laugh, since this investigation was being handled by me—a human who was not *their own* and never would be—and Jordan, the least discreet person on the planet. We were like a double whammy. A one-two punch. A not-so-dynamic duo.

Nevertheless, I was determined to get the job done.

So we took an Uber, Jordan chattering to the driver—who happened to be a Wonderful Mug customer—all the way. I had him drop us a good half mile away from the attack site, just in case.

Dark had already fallen, but the streetlights cast a wan light on the street. As we walked up the hill toward the spot, Jordan looked around brightly. "Wow. This is way different from my pack's compound, or even the Howling Residence. Guess some people have a lot of money, huh?"

"You could say that," I said, eyeing a house with at least four levels, most of them fronted with glass. I put my hand out to slow him down as we approached the trees. "That's the place. Are you picking up anything?"

Jordan's eyes lost focus and his nostrils quivered. "Yeah. I can smell Lachlan. And fish. And something else, but—hey, there's a squirrel!"

"Jordan. Focus. Please."

"Right. Sorry." He bit his lip. "I could be more accurate if I shifted. Do you think anyone would notice?"

A wolf in an upscale Portland neighborhood? "What do you think?"

He brightened. "You could pretend to be walking your dog."

"I'm pretty sure anybody with half an eye will be able to figure out that a wolf is not a German Shepherd."

Jordan tilted his head, and for an instant his sardonic expression made him look older than his twenty-one years— like an adult rather than an overgrown teenager. "You got any better ideas?"

I sighed. "Fine." He started to take off his jacket, but I held up a hand. "How about you wait to strip off until we're under cover of the trees, okay? Even if we can pass your wolf off as a friendly pooch, I doubt a naked guy morphing into said pooch would escape comment."

Even in the sketchy light, I could tell he was blushing. "Sorry. I forget sometimes. Humaning is really hard. I don't know how you do it."

As I trailed him into the copse, I forbore from saying I didn't have much choice. Once we were shielded from sight, he didn't waste any time, shedding his clothes faster than I could change lenses. I very carefully did *not* watch him, busying myself with collecting his discarded garments and folding them up to fit in my pack.

When I looked up, wolf-Jordan was gazing up at me with the same big brown puppy eyes as human-Jordan. He gave a short yip and then bent his head to the ground. As I followed him out of the trees and down the street, I really *really* hoped that the thief hadn't had a getaway car stashed in a convenient cul-de-sac, because I doubted even Jordan's super-sniffer powers would be up to a car chase.

With a low whine in the back of his throat, Jordan picked up speed, making me trot to keep up. Ears pricked, he made a last dash and stopped, panting with a wolfy smile.

Right in front of the Martinson's pretentious wrought-iron gates.

And call me a cynic, but I wasn't surprised in the least.

# CHAPTER TWELVE

"Swell," I muttered. "Now what?"

Jordan dashed behind one of the massive rhododendrons that flanked the gate, and from the way the foliage rustled, I guessed he was shifting back to human form. "It's in there."

"Are you sure? I mean, it *was* here. Lachlan showed up carrying the thing earlier today."

He poked his head out from between the dusty leaves and held out his hand so I could pass him his clothes. "No. It's definitely here now. I could scent the residual trail from earlier, but this is fresher. Stronger. Besides, if it had been taken away, there'd be another trail leaving, and there isn't. It's definitely here."

I set my bag next to my feet and leaned around the stone gate post to peer at the house. Two cars were drawn up in front of the door, a sports car—red, because of course it would be red—and a sleek black town car. What were the chances I could just buzz the intercom and ask for a few words with the Martinsons: "Pardon me, but did you ambush Lachlan Brodie and steal his pack?" Yeah, that would go over well. "It may be here," I told Jordan, "but I have no idea how we can get in."

Jordan grinned. "We could always dig under the fence. Digging's the other thing I'm good at."

"I don't think digging under a stone fence is an option."

"Then what? Just say abracadabra or open sesame?"

The gates began to swing outward, smoothly and without a creak.

I stared from the gates—now wide open—to Jordan. "That can't be—" The front door of the mansion crashed open and Reid stormed out onto the porch, his black overcoat flaring behind him. He dove down the stairs, heading toward the sports car.

Pierce appeared in the doorway in a black overcoat identical to his son's. "Reid! Have a care. A rash action now could ruin everything."

Reid flung open the car door. "I know what I'm doing, Father. Believe it or not, I always have. And I'm done waiting to claim what's mine."

Jordan made a face. "That doesn't sound good."

"You know what else doesn't sound good? Getting caught spying on them. Duck!"

Jordan disappeared under his bush as I snagged my bag and edged behind its twin on the other side of the gate. We needn't have taken that much care—Reid bombed out of the driveway and onto the road without even pausing. I was about to ease out of hiding—a branch was poking me in the side—when the town car purred through the gates. It at least paused to check for traffic, but the tinted windows were too dark for me to see who was inside. I assumed it was Pierce, since he'd been dressed for going out when I spotted him in the doorway, but—

"Hssst! Hugh!"

I peered through the screen of rhododendron leaves to see Jordan gesturing madly at the open gates. As the town car slid smoothly onto the street, the gates began to close and Jordan darted through them.

"Jordan, what the— Crap," I muttered. I glanced over my shoulder at the town car's disappearing taillights. I doubted my probationary period would survive a trespassing charge, but I could hardly leave Jordan in there on his own. My bag caught on a branch as I lunged out to follow him. I cursed under my breath, but I couldn't get it loose. With the gap narrowing by the second, however, I let go and nipped through just before the opening got too small. If somebody stole it from behind the bush, I could replace it. But if I let Jordan get caught by the Martinsons? Not exactly something I could put on an expense report.

Jordan at least had the sense not to walk straight up the drive. For all I knew, the Martinsons had security cameras covering every inch of the property. "At least they don't have guard dogs," I groused as I hurried to catch up to Jordan, where he was skulking along the fence.

"This is so awesome!" he whispered. "I've always wanted to do surveillance, just like you."

"Jordan, this isn't surveillance. This is trespassing."

He blinked at me, his eyes huge in the dark. "But the gate was open."

"No. The gate was closing. Probably to keep people like us out."

"But, Hugh, Mr. Brodie's pack is *in there* and it doesn't belong to them. Isn't it the right thing to do to get it back?"

I scrubbed my hands through my hair. "No, they shouldn't have Lachlan's pack, and the fact that they do is damning. But *somebody* called the SMTs to pick Lachlan up. Maybe it was them and they intend to return the pack once he's released from the hospital."

Jordan just stared at me. Yeah, I didn't believe that either. With all the bad blood between Lachlan and Reid—personified by the man they apparently both wanted—it was entirely possible that Reid had taken the pack for leverage against Lachlan. I doubted he was the type to resist temptation if it hit him right between the eyes.

"Look, we should contact Mal. The supe council polices this type of—"

"Hugh!" He grabbed my arm and shook it. "Look! It's a jar."

I peered through the gloom. "What jar? What does a jar—"

"No. The *door*. It's a*jar*."

"Just because a door isn't latched, we can't just waltz—"

Too late. He darted across the manicured grass and skirted the geometrically precise hedge to cross the flagstone patio. Grinning, he pushed the French door open with one finger.

"Jordan, don't be a—" He slipped inside. "Fabulous. Now it's not just trespassing. It's B & E."

But I had no chance to convince him to leave if I stayed out here, and this was Jordan, the kid who hadn't gone a day at Wonderful Mug without breaking something, including himself. I could hardly let him bang around in the house alone. He might end up burning the place down.

"I am gonna be so fired," I muttered as I sprinted across the lawn and slipped inside. At least we hadn't ended up in that creepy-ass study.

This room was dim, lit only by the embers of a dying fire in a huge fireplace. It wasn't nearly as cluttered as the rest of the house. In fact, it was practically empty, with only a few tall, thin objects lurking in the shadowy corners, as if this was the place the Martinsons sent their old coat racks to die.

Across the room, a door opened, silhouetting Jordan against a brighter hallway light. I headed toward him, but as I crossed the bare wooden floor, I realized it wasn't as bare as I thought: The light picked out a metal inlay.

There was a pentagram embedded in the floor. And those dead coat racks? Candelabra. Six foot tall wrought iron candelabra topped with black candles as thick as my wrist.

Holy crap. Pierce Martinson was an elemental mage, and this must be his workroom.

I wasn't as worried about getting fired now as I was about getting dead.

"Hugh, come on! It's this way!" Jordan disappeared out the door. I hurried after him, although I can admit that my rush wasn't entirely because I needed to keep him in check. I didn't want to spend any more time in that workroom than I had to.

Believe me, I don't object to pentagrams and magic accouterments on principle. Heck, we had several slate-floored, slate-walled chambers at the Quest offices for magical ceremonies and rituals. The whole building used to belong to a witches' collective, so it stood to reason. But as a human, I was never allowed inside when the spells were being cast.

You've got to know by now that at the hint of anything supernatural, I'm so there. But intruding into a magical working uninvited? Even I'm not that stupid. Not after Zeke told me AJ's story.

AJ had been summoned and bound into service, passed from magician to magician, until he'd tricked his last master—a necromancer, and you *never* wanted to mess with jokers who wielded magic powered by death—and escaped. Apparently, if any magical chamber wasn't carefully cleansed after each use—something Zeke was absolutely meticulous about at Quest—the spells could leave residue. And since a lot of those spells were aimed at human victims—or included human, er, components—everyone, including me, agreed it would be best for me to stay out.

I poked my head into the hallway, checking for movement and listening hard. Pierce and Reid might be gone, but there was still Eleri, the thorny maid, to consider, let alone any other servants. And Wyn, of course. He hadn't been on the porch with Pierce and Reid, and hadn't been in the sports car. He *might* have come out after Jordan and I hid, since the fence blocked our view of the house, and climbed into the town car with Pierce, his father-in-law-to-be.

But he could just as easily still be here.

However, the only movement I could detect was Jordan creeping up a narrow stairway at the end of the hall—the servants' stairs?—and the only sound his footsteps on the bare wooden treads.

I crept after him as soundlessly as I could, hoping Eleri wasn't waiting at the top, ready to wrap us both in brambles.

But Jordan scooted out into a wide, empty corridor. He glanced over his shoulder at me, his face practically glowing with glee. He pointed toward the second door on the left, a room that would overlook the front of the house.

*"It's in there,"* he mouthed.

I managed to grab his arm before he opened the door. "We need to leave. Now."

"But, Hugh, we can't go without the pack. That's why we're here. Packs are *important*."

I lifted an eyebrow. "This is a backpack, Jordan. Not a bunch of affiliated werewolves."

"I know that," he said indignantly. "But we have to take it back to him. It's the right thing to do."

Spectral spiders staged a line dance up my spine, the urge to bolt nearly overpowering. But really, what choice did I have? I had no illusion that if Pierce Martinson wanted to find out who'd been traipsing through his house unannounced, he could do it with one puff of magical smoke or whatever. No matter how you sliced it, though, the Martinsons had no right to Lachlan's property, and neither did Wyn. He'd renounced that right when he'd demanded the sundering.

"Can you tell if the room is empty?" I murmured.

Jordan sniffed experimentally, and his brow knotted. "Yeah. In fact, it's *really* empty. Like there's nothing in there but furniture and the pack, even though somebody was staying there pretty recently."

"You can tell all that by smell? From out here?" He gave me a *Get real, dude* look. "Okay then. Let's get it and get out before somebody asks us what the hell we're doing here uninvited." And I sincerely hoped that this counted as something that fell under the "better to ask forgiveness than permission" category.

Because at this rate, we were gonna need a boatload of forgiveness. Some of it from a magician who specialized in fire.

# CHAPTER THIRTEEN

Jordan opened the door sloooowly, but it didn't creak any more than the well-oiled gates had, and we snuck inside. The room—a suite, really, with a king-sized bed, a sitting area tucked into a bay window, and an ensuite bathroom which, just from the glimpse I got of its marble tiles and free-standing clawfoot tub, was bigger than my kitchen and dining room put together.

The place was gorgeous, even in the dim moonlight shining in through the windows, its carpets thick and plush, its ceilings high, and its walls notably devoid of formerly living wildlife. Nevertheless, there was something about it—a coldness maybe, which was pretty ironic since we were burgling a fire mage's house—that raised the hair on my arms.

While I was goggling at how the other half lived, Jordan darted over to a tall, ornately carved wardrobe and opened its mirrored door.

"Here it is!" he called, hefting the pack out by one strap.

"Jordan," I whispered urgently, "keep it down. Do you *want* to be discovered?"

He winced. "Oops. Sorry." Then he grinned, although it wobbled as he glanced over his shoulder. "I don't like this place. Can we go now?"

I stared gloomily out the window at the closed gates. "That's debatable."

If even Jordan was uneasy, I didn't want to waste any more time inside. I took the pack from him—no sense tempting fate more than we already had—and gestured for him to precede me. I closed the door softly behind me and followed him down the corridor, but when he reached the stairs, he froze like a hunting dog scenting game.

He turned toward me, wide-eyed. *Someone's here,* he mouthed, jerking his thumb at the ceiling.

Right on cue, a board creaked above our heads. I wasn't about to find out if it was Wyn or Eleri. I held a finger across my lips and shooed Jordan onward, and for a wonder, he got the message and crept soundlessly down the stairs. I wasn't quite as lucky—one stair creaked loudly under my foot halfway down and I froze, wishing heartily for the plush carpet from the bedroom suite.

When nobody thundered down the stairs after me, though, I unfroze myself and tiptoed down the rest of the flight. I really didn't want to cross that workroom again, but what choice did we have? It was the only door we knew for certain was open.

I didn't take a full breath until we were outside. Jordan was about to sprint across the patio, but I held him back, checking above us for any lights that might indicate a watcher in an upstairs window. But no telltale rectangles of light fell across the lawn. That was either a good thing or a bad thing—good, if it meant the person upstairs faced away from this side of the house; bad if they *were* on this side of the house, because it was much easier to see out from a darkened room than a lighted one.

But again, we didn't have much choice. So we both raced for the fence and pushed behind the aggressively trimmed hedge, doing enough damage that the gardeners wouldn't thank us the next time they arrived to bushwhack the plants into shapes not found in nature, but not enough to be too obvious to a casual observer.

Luckily for us—and the plants—there was enough of a gap between them and the fence that we could edge our way along, our backs to the rough stone, without making more ruckus than an elk stampede, although since I couldn't sling Lachlan's pack on my back, it whacked against my knee at every other step. Either his seal skin was lumpier than it had looked, or he carried other stuff in here. Probably rocks by the weight.

We made it to the gateposts without raising an outcry, but then we faced the other problem.

The gates.

"Uh oh," Jordan said. "Now what?"

I took a deep breath. "This is why we need to consider the consequences of our actions and make a plan *before* barging forward.. Never go into someplace unless you know how you can get out again."

He bit his lip. "I guess that would be a good idea, huh?" He rose on his toes and peered over the hedge. "We could just wait here until one of those cars comes back. I mean, they have to come home sometime, right?"

"In theory. However, I expect they'd notice if somebody scampered behind the car to dodge out of the gates. It's different from the other direction—they're not here to see us. But when they come in, well, here they are. We'd be hard to miss, especially if the car that comes back first is that town car. It probably takes five minutes just to clear the gates."

*Wait a minute.*

Rich people—or the Martinsons specifically—didn't strike me as anyone who'd want to trouble themselves to actually punch a button to open or close their gates from the inside. In fact, the reason they'd been standing open earlier today was probably so they wouldn't be bothered by the dang things opening and closing—and possibly setting off an alarm—when the gardeners were mucking around in the underbrush.

I popped my head above the hedge to take a look and *aha!* Just as I thought. A discreet little unit about one and a half town car lengths from the gate that probably contained a motion sensor. To activate it, I'd need to emerge into the open, at least for a little while, but it beat the alternative—aka parking ourselves behind the bushes and hoping we didn't get nabbed at some unspecified future moment when one of the Martinsons decided to come home.

And incidentally, if I had my choice about which one to face down? I'd pick Reid. Yeah, he had a hair-trigger temper and although we were roughly the same size, his weight was proportionally distributed more to muscle mass than mine was, but the only other advantage he had over me was money, and that made a lousy weapon in a fist fight.

Pierce, on the other hand, could probably set me on fire.

I nudged Jordan aside. "I'm going to try something. If it works and the gates open, run. I'll be right behind you."

Big-eyed, Jordan nodded.

I kept low, blessing my boring wardrobe that consisted of mostly dark jeans and T-shirts. My jacket wasn't a fancy duster overcoat like the Martinsons sported, but North Face fleece was way more discreet: less fabric to flap in the breeze, which had definitely picked up, and no sheen to reflect the moonlight. It's a good thing Jordan wasn't still scampering around naked or he'd be a hazard on both fronts—although in his case, the articles flapping in the breeze wouldn't be fabric.

The sensor was in two parts—a transmitter that emitted a light beam on one side and a receiver on the other. Presumably, I only needed to disrupt the beam for the gates to open. I passed my hand in front of it. Nothing. I heaved an exasperated sigh. Could it be disabled somehow? Smart enough to detect when the Martinson's cars were on premises as opposed to out and about?

Or maybe…

I hefted Lachlan's pack, holding it above the beam and then lowering it slowly and holding it in place. I counted in my head. *One one thousand. Two one thousand. Three—*

And the gates swung open.

Jordan, following instructions for a change, darted out as soon as the gap was wide enough. I kept the bag in place for another couple of *one thousands*, just in case, then raced for freedom. We made it—barely—out onto the street, where I had to put my head down, hands on my knees. Man, I was *so* not cut out for a life of crime.

I untangled my bag from the bush and then motioned for Jordan to follow me as I jogged toward the copse again. Once inside the tree screen, I turned to him.

"Listen, I want to thank you for helping me."

He beamed. "No problem, Hugh. I—"

"But if you *ever* do anything like that again, I'll...I'll...I'll sic Dr. MacLeod on you."

His eyes rounded. "You wouldn't."

"I would. And more. The supe community might police its own, but we just broke *human* laws, and since the Martinsons look human, appear human, *pass* for human, they could call the cops on us right freaking now. And they'd be within their rights."

"B-but they took Lachlan's pack."

I lifted an eyebrow. "Yeah, try explaining that to one of our officers in blue. It still counts as stealing, Jordan, even if you're stealing something back. And since there was somebody in the house when we were there? That raises things another notch." I blotted my damp forehead with my sleeve. "At least we weren't armed."

"Oh!" he said brightly, and pulled a folded knife the length of my hand out of his pocket. "I had my knife with me. I didn't know if we'd need it."

My knees wobbled, and not just from the notion of anyone allowing Jordan a knife. "I'm glad I didn't know that beforehand. Now." I looped the strap of my bag over my shoulder and shrugged into Lachlan's pack. "I'll return this to Lachlan. You. Go home."

His face fell. "Don't you need help carrying both those bags? I don't mind."

"Neither one of us should stay around here any longer. Please, Jordan. Go home. And *stay* there."

"Okay," he said, lower lip trembling.

"Do you need a token for the FTA?"

He perked up a little at that. "Oh no." He brandished his cell phone. "I've got Hector's app. I'm good. I can call a ride for you too, if you want."

"No thanks. Quest covers my rides." Besides, I didn't want to break any more laws tonight, and I was pretty sure that app wasn't fully sanctioned. However, I'd leave any required ass-kicking to Bryce. I pulled a rather crumpled oak leaf out of my pocket, pressed my thumb to the golden rune in its center, and murmured, "Cludo."

The driver who showed up wasn't my usual guy, which wasn't surprising since this wasn't my usual time or place. This one was a slender barefoot person with longish brown hair twined with leaves. They took one look at me and and their green eyes narrowed and their mouth pursed as if they'd been sucking a lemon. Beyond their shoulder, Jordan widened his eyes and mouthed *dryad*.

Terrific. Apparently my popularity with dryads had spread— probably through the literal grapevine. I heaved a sigh. "St. Stupid's please."

The dryad sniffed, although I doubted it was for the same reason Jordan did. Usually I try to chat with my driver on the way through Faerie—I mean, it's only polite, right? Besides, the best way to learn about all the different fae species is straight from the horse's—or fae's—mouth, as it were. The dryad wasn't inclined to chat, and that was just as well. They deposited me at St. Stupid's and popped back through the portal without a word.

I sighed again as I headed out to the reception desk. I'd have to speak to Bryce about the general dryad hate-fest. They all practically worshipped the ground he walked on—him being an environmental science professor as well as a druid—so he'd know how I could make amends. I mean, I don't *have* to have everyone like me, but having an entire supe species gunning for me was a little alarming. If the dryads ever decided to weaponize their annoyance, I'd never be sure whether my spider plant might strangle me one day.

Maybe I should stick to plastic plants for a while.

Renee was still at the desk. I smiled at her—hey, I'm a friendly guy, okay? "I'm here to see Lachlan Brodie again."

She blinked up at me. "I'm sorry, but he's checked out."

I goggled at her. Lachlan's pack slid off my shoulder and pulled my elbow down. "Checked out? But I thought he needed additional treatment." Not to mention he'd sent me on an errand that required me to break several human laws and possibly put me and Jordan in the crosshairs of an elemental mage. The least he could do was wait for me to report back. My ears started to burn the way they always did when I got angry.

Now, I'm a pretty even-tempered guy, but that doesn't mean I'll take everything lying down. The least Lachlan could have done was call me and let me know he'd gone. I didn't even know where to find him.

"Matt?"

I froze. Only three people ever called me Matt. Ted, his husband, and—

David Evans-Kendrick bustled over from the elevator and gave me a hug. "You're looking well. What are you doing here?"

David's an *achubydd*, one of those magical healers I was telling you about, although a couple of years ago, he thought he was as human as I am. He's also married to one of the scariest fae warriors in existence, Lord Alun Kendrick, who also happens to be the psychologist for the supe community.

If David was here, that explained why St. Stupid's would allow Lachlan to leave. "I came to see a client. Lachlan Brodie. I'm guessing since you're here—"

"Oh yes," David said sunnily. "He's all better." A wrinkle puckered his forehead. "Nasty business. Not only a subdural hematoma but some kind of magical binding."

"Binding? You mean like a curse?"

David glanced sidelong at Renee. "Let's go somewhere and chat, shall we?" I followed him through the busy ER to what appeared to be a staff lounge, currently unpopulated, where he spun to face me. "Lachlan's a Quest client?"

I nodded. "He was the victim of harassment and low-key vandalism." I hefted Lachlan's pack. "Not to mention the mugging and theft."

David chewed on his lower lip. "I'm not sure, mind, but I think he might be a victim of more than that. Not just physical attacks, but metaphysical as well."

"You mean magical?"

David nodded. "His injuries—hematoma, the amount of time he was unconscious... Well, let's say they're troubling."

"I imagine any kind of head trauma would be."

"Yes. If there were evidence of head trauma."

My eyes widened. "You mean he wasn't bashed on the head? But he had that lump."

David shook his head. "From what I can tell, the symptoms, including the knot on his noggin, were all induced magically."

That rocked me back on my heels. *Achubyddion* and witches and druids and the other medimagical staff at St. Stupid's *healed* with magic, but I'd never heard of anyone doing the opposite. "Could an elemental mage do something like that?"

David screwed up his face. "Ugh. Mages are...problematic. You know how witches are constrained by natural consequences and druids by the balance of nature?" I nodded. "Mages don't have that kind of failsafe. The only limits on them are the properties of their element."

"So a fire mage couldn't cause a flood?"

"Theoretically, no. Although there are work-arounds. Not so many now that the Realm Accords have granted full rights to the Host and made it illegal for anyone to summon and bind them to service."

The Host. That's how demons and angels were referred to now. I hefted Lachlan's pack again. "I just…liberated this from Pierce Martinson's house. It's Lachlan's. It was taken when he was attacked."

"Holy cats!" David's eyebrows disappeared under his bangs. "A fire mage? I don't know exactly how he could have managed Lachlan's injuries without leaving burns, but I suppose it's possible. I don't really know much about mages. They're kinda at odds with the supe council." He wrinkled his nose again. "Probably because they're not allowed to enslave any poor demons anymore. Not that they were supposed to do it before, but somehow they always found a way to justify themselves." He snorted. "They're worse than Republican congressional representatives."

"I really need to return this to Lachlan. Do you know where he went after you treated him?"

"He didn't really say, but Wyn mentioned the boat."

My stomach jolted. "Wyn? Wyn Ellis was here?"

David nodded. "He's Lachlan's husband, so he's on the hospital's emergency contact form. Why?"

"Because Wyn's—" Gah! Client confidentiality. "I can't say. But they mentioned the boat?" I reached for another FTA token, but my pocket held nothing but leaf crumbs. Damn. I needed to get back to the Quest offices and replenish my supply. Unfortunately, while the portal from our office could get me to St. Stupid's with no FTA driver, the reverse wasn't true. "Thanks for the intel, David. I've got to go."

I raced out of the hospital, my phone already in my hand to call an Uber. I blinked at the time on the screen. Jeez, it was almost midnight. How had it gotten so late? I ought to be exhausted—this had been a very long and eventful day—but the adrenaline spike that had kept me going since Lachlan's phone call didn't fade in the ten-minute ride to Quest.

As I leaped out of the Uber and pounded up the stairs, I hoped like hell that Lachlan would still be alive when I found him.

Because I wanted the pleasure of murdering the idiot myself.

# CHAPTER FOURTEEN

When the FTA driver—not my usual guy again, but not a dryad either—delivered me to the woods outside Ted's cave, I didn't even stop to hang out inside the way I normally did to... well...moon over Ted, I guess you could call it. Instead, I plunged down the hillside, Lachlan's pack bouncing painfully on my back and my own bag smacking me on the hip with every stride.

I'd never been so relieved to reach my little one-bedroom rental house and spot my dusty Honda parked in its usual spot, its hood scattered with brown leaves from the oak tree in the neighbor's yard. I tossed the pack in the trunk and got in, setting my bag on the passenger seat. The car started up first thing—it might be unlovely, but it was reliable—and I tore out on the road from Dewton to the marina.

Once again, it didn't take long. The traffic was sparse, even though one jerk decided I wasn't going fast enough and passed me on the blind curve leading to the bay. When I reached the marina, the parking lot was empty except for Lachlan's truck in its usual spot, so I cut the lights on the Honda and parked a good distance away from the boat.

There were lights in the cabin.

Months of surveillance experience kicked in as I made sure my dome lights were turned off before grabbing my camera and climbing out of my car. I didn't close the door all the way, just pushed it to so it wouldn't make a noise. Keeping low, I crept along the dock until I could get a clear view through the starboard windows.

Lachlan was there, all right. So was Wyn, and they were looking pretty dang cozy, if you get my drift. No—not *that* drift. But they were standing close together, Wyn gazing up at Lachlan and Lachlan down at Wyn. Wyn's back was to me, so I couldn't see his expression, but I could see Lachlan's, and it was like a punch to the gut.

I'd seen that same tenderness on Ted's face whenever he looked at Quentin, on Mal's when he thought of Bryce, on Niall's when he had Gareth on his mind, on Zeke's when he was on his way home to Hamish.

Lachlan took Wyn's hand in his and pressed something into it, closing Wyn's fingers around it and engulfing Wyn's smaller fist in his own. I backed away. Were they planning to take things…further? The fish-infused berth made any onboard shenanigans unlikely, but what if they headed back to their apartment or to some other cozy hideaway to, er, consummate their reconciliation?

"I'm not about to surveil *that*," I muttered. But I took enough shots of the boat and the lot as evidence for terminating Lachlan's contract. As I backed away, ready to return to my car, a wave rocked the boat, and the moonlight caught on something that I hadn't noticed before.

There, on the transom, right over the lettering that spelled out the boat's name—*Cridhe na Mara*—someone had nailed a split and gutted fish.

My ears started to burn again. Seriously? Lachlan could canoodle when the evidence of Wyn's perfidy was right there—nailed to his precious boat.

One of Quest's contractual requirements in taking a case was complete transparency on the part of our clients, for their benefit as well as ours. Lachlan had signed that contract, but clearly there were a few pertinent details he hadn't shared with us, with *me*. Had he been intending to use our investigation as leverage to convince Wyn to come back to him? That seemed pretty far-fetched, yet the result—Wyn back on the boat with him—couldn't be denied. Had he manufactured the whole thing, made Quest complicit—hell, turned me into a *cat burglar* —just to save his marriage? Was he really *that* selfish and manipulative?

"I bet his seal skin isn't even in the damn pack," I growled as I photographed the latest herring. And suddenly I had to know. I stalked back to the Honda and pulled the pack out of the trunk. I may have slammed it *and* the door too after I tossed the pack inside and climbed behind the wheel, because I didn't really care if he knew I was here. Not that he'd probably notice. Not with Wyn taking up all his attention.

I unzipped the pack's largest compartment and something soft and black practically exploded out of it, spilling over my lap and onto the floor. I didn't turn on the dome light, but I didn't need it to tell this wasn't any damn seal skin. Not with lapels, silky lining, and a label sewn in the back under the collar.

I took a deep, shaky breath, trying to tamp down my anger. There was a lot I didn't know about the supernatural community yet, but nothing I'd read indicated that the seal skin could shift its appearance without the selkie inside. In fact, that was one of the reasons selkies back in the day got captured so easily, with all those nosy fishermen finding their discarded skins on the beach.

"He *played* me," I growled. Had he just been trying to get me out of the way until the hospital contacted Wyn and he could play the sympathy card on the path to make-up sex? If that was so, he didn't have to call me. After the Martinson interview debacle, I'd chalked the case up as done and dusted and never expected to hear from Lachlan Brodie again. I'd half expected him to refuse to pay his bill.

If I wasn't afraid of what I'd interrupt—there were some things I really didn't need to see—I'd have confronted Lachlan right this moment. But I wasn't a full-fledged investigator yet, nor was I fully invested by the council. I'd let Mal handle cutting Lachlan loose, as well as imposing whatever penalty was appropriate for this kind of infraction.

I shoved the key in the ignition, but before I could turn the engine over, another car squealed into the lot. It zoomed diagonally across the pitted tarmac and skidded to a stop right in front of *Cridhe na Mara*, the headlights illuminating that poor crucified fish. I recognized the car—it was Reid Martinson's red sports car, last seen peeling out of his driveway. I blinked. *Scratch that.* Last seen barreling past me on that blind corner and nearly sending me into the hillside, the big jerk. Since he hadn't made it here before me, he'd probably swung past Wyn and Lachlan's apartment first if—I had to tamp down a wave of revulsion—Wyn was who he was seeking to "claim."

Reid climbed out of the car and slammed his door even louder than I had. He strode toward the boat's gangway, his footsteps pounding hollowly on the wooden dock, but he didn't climb aboard.

"Lachlan Brodie!" he bellowed. "Show yourself."

I half-expected Lachlan to ignore him. After all, he'd gotten what he wanted, hadn't he? He and Wyn could just sail away and leave Reid to rage alone. But he climbed out on deck and faced Reid across the narrow band of water that separated the boat from the dock, his arms crossed over his chest, his jaw like granite.

One thing I knew for certain: Based solely on today's experiences, as an ordinary working-class human, I had no business getting in the middle of a supe brawl. My Quest credentials were a pretty flimsy shield against feral dryads, high-powered magicians, and/or people with more money than I'd ever see in my life. Call me a coward, but regardless of my fascination with the supernatural, I had no desire to be collateral damage in one of their firefights. I loved my job, but I wasn't ready to die for it.

I ignored the knots in my belly as I started the Honda. It couldn't be regret. I refused to allow it. I'd had enough of that to last me a lifetime, and I wasn't about to sign up for another stint in the lovelorn column.

Lachlan and Reid didn't stop hollering at each other—or rather, Reid didn't stop hollering, and Lachlan let it roll off him like water off a seal's skin.

*Seal skin.*

I wondered if it was tucked away on his boat somewhere, after all. I wondered if he'd ever bother to reclaim the pack he'd begged me to retrieve, even though it didn't contain what he'd contended. Well, he could damn well take a little jaunt to the Quest offices and retrieve it from Zeke, because once I filed my report, I was done with Lachlan Brodie.

I drove back to my place and parked the Honda. Dead oak leaves swirled into a little spiral and dropped onto the hood, even as I was trying to stuff the coat back into the pack.

Wonderful. Now the feral dryad brigade was apparently weaponizing leaves. I didn't know if they could insinuate their twiggy fingers into the engine or puncture the tires or jam the locks, but I couldn't be bothered now. "Knock yourselves out," I muttered and headed up the hill to the cave for an FTA pickup.

If they vandalized my car, I'd deal with it. That's what I did. That's what I'd always done, whether the problem was scaring up my next freelance photography gig or nursing a broken heart.

I stopped in the clearing in front of the cave, but before I could pull out my FTA token, my cell phone rang with an unknown number. I punched the answer icon with probably unnecessary force. "Hello?"

"Is this...Lachlan's friend?" The voice, a broken whisper, was almost too soft to hear. "From the dock?"

"Yes," I said cautiously.

"It's not you. Thank goodness it's not you. I didn't think it was you. The coat was wrong. But I was afraid..."

Something about the wavery voice was familiar. "Blair?"

"Yeah," they said. "Can you come to Lachlan's boat slip? Please?"

"I was just there. Has something happened?"

Blair's gulp was more audible than their voice had been. "Yes. Hurry." The line went dead.

My belly tumbled to my knees. *Crap.* Was the kid in trouble? Had Reid and Lachlan's feud escalated? I tossed Lachlan's pack into the cave. I kept my bag—I might need the camera or one of my other tools, but there was no point hauling that heavy, lumpy, *worthless* pack around.

As I bombed down the hill, stumbling badly more than once in the wan moonlight, I realized that physical baggage wasn't my only problem. My heart wouldn't be pounding this hard, my stomach wouldn't be tied quite so tightly, if I were as indifferent to Lachlan as I told myself I ought to be.

*Double crap.*

Luckily, the dryads hadn't bothered with anything more than dead leaves and enough pine sap on the windshield to make my wipers struggle in the next rain. I gunned the Honda onto 101 and broke the speed limit all the way to the dock. When I barreled into the lot, at first I thought I'd gotten the wrong slip because *Cridhe na Mara* wasn't bobbing in the water where I expected it to be. But Reid's car was still parked where it had been when I left, and I spotted Blair, huddled next to a bollard.

I screeched to a halt and shoved the door open the instant the engine juddered off. "Blair?" I called as I climbed out. "It's Matt. I mean Hugh. I mean Lachlan's…friend."

Blair took a half step forward, their arms wrapped so tightly across their middle it looked as though they were wearing an army-issued straight jacket. Their jaunty rainbow beanie was gone, their long hair whipping across their face in the wind off the water. They didn't say anything. Just pointed.

Into the water.

Heart in my throat, I hurried forward, chanting *please no please no please no* with every step. But when I peered over the edge of the dock, it wasn't Lachlan's body—in human or seal form—or even Wyn who floated there, lifeless, in a flare of sodden black overcoat.

It was Reid Martinson.

# CHAPTER FIFTEEN

I dialed Zeke on our emergency line as I was stripping off my coat. He answered on the first ring because of course he did—demon super speed was one of the abilities Zeke's Sheol progenitor had baked into him—not that actual *baking* was involved. That I knew of, anyway, but, you know, *Sheol*. Lava rivers and all that.

"Hugh? What's wrong?"

"I need you to get the SMTs down to Lachlan Brodie's boat slip on the Nehalem River, stat. Reid Martinson's face down in the water. I don't know for how long. I'm going in now to try to pull him out."

"Hugh!" Zeke's voice, usually so friendly and well-modulated, was sharp. "Do *not* go into that water. Do *not* touch Reid's body. Stay where you are and...and do your job."

"My job?" I barked. "What, just take freaking *pictures*? He might still be revivable, but not if I don't get him out—"

"You're human, Hugh. *Matt*." Zeke's pleading tone stopped me in the act of jumping off the pier. "And this is a supe affair. You don't know what led to Reid being in the water and there could be...ramifications. You need to leave the situation to those who are qualified to handle it."

I stared down at Reid's body. The river wasn't the most pristine—a discarded water bottle bumped against his outflung hand, a dead fish floated belly up by his foot, and a mat of seaweed tangled with his hair. It seemed wrong to leave him there.

But I wasn't *qualified*. Most of the supe community barely tolerated me. I heaved a shaky breath. "There's something else. Lachlan's boat is missing. And I saw Lachlan and Wyn on it earlier. Lachlan and Reid had an…an argument."

Zeke sucked in an audible breath. "I'll let them know. For now, please document the scene."

"Right." I bent slowly to pick up my jacket. "Document. Because that's my *job*."

"Matt," Zeke's voice was gentle. If he was still calling me *Matt*, he was probably trying to ground me and prevent me from doing something stupid. "What you do is important. We all have our places, okay? The things we do best. The things that matter. And we couldn't run this place without you."

Headlights swept across the parking lot, half-blinding me, and I realized that Blair had disappeared at some point. "I think somebody's here."

"That will be the SMTs."

I squinted through the glare. "In an ambulance? How did they get here so fast?"

"Local resources. We put them in place during the spread of Hrodgar's Syndrome. Dr. Kendrick will be there soon, along with Pierce Martinson, so you might want to—"

"Get in, get it done, and get out?"

"It might be best," he said apologetically as the SMTs jumped out of the ambulance. One of them, a tall Black man with a high-top fade and a gray parrot on his shoulder, strode over to me.

"The victim?" he asked, although he seemed efficient, not dismissive.

"Down there."

He turned his head toward the parrot. "Zuri?" She launched herself off his shoulder and glided out over the water, circling Reid's body, as the SMT and his smaller white partner raced for the pier almost faster than I could track.

I stood back and let them do their jobs.

"Matt? Are you still there?" Zeke's voice sounded distant.

Aaaand that would be because I'd let my hand fall to my side, my phone still in a death grip. I winced. Maybe not the best choice of words. I lifted the phone to my ear. "I'm here."

"I've checked with Mal. He'd like you to return to the office as soon as you've finished with the photographs. He'll debrief with you then."

"Got it. See you."

I hung up and got with the program. I concentrated on the parking lot and the dock and its surroundings, because I really didn't want to watch as the SMTs pulled Reid's limp body out of the water.

I know what you're thinking. Why did I call Zeke and not 9-1-1? Why not get the ME out here along with the police to investigate the...murder and take charge of the body?

Why? Secrecy Pact, remember? Supes police supes. I can understand it, you know? Can you imagine what would happen if an ME did an autopsy on a vampire? Or if a junior werewolf got picked up on a drunk and disorderly and had an uncontrolled shift in the county lockup?

The dangers run both ways, so I get it. I do. But I'd spent thirty-seven years immersed in, and sometimes skirting, the American—*human* American—legal system. Was it so surprising that it shook me to witness something that defied those laws?

The SMTs laid Reid out on the dock and worked over him—the two of them assisted by the parrot, who must be the first guy's familiar. Another man had joined them while I'd been talking to Zeke, a tall white man who reminded me of the guy who won *The Great British Baking Show* a couple of years ago. The new guy had Reid's hand in his, but as I watched, he laid it over Reid's chest and shook his head. Reid's body remained still, unmoving. The three of them sat back and stared at one another bleakly.

I edged toward them. "I don't want to intrude, but I'm with Quest and I've been instructed to document the scene?"

The guy with the parrot glanced up at me and I braced myself for blowback, but he just nodded tiredly. "Of course. You're Hugh, right? You made the call?" I nodded. "I'm Ky, by the way. My familiar, Zuri." He gestured to his partner. "Pete." He stripped off his nitrile glove and draped an arm across the third man's shoulders. "My boyfriend, Ewan. *Achubydd.*"

Ewan was like David, then. I met Ewan's gaze as he leaned into Ky. "No calon spark?"

Ewan shook his head again. "He's gone."

"My boy!" The tortured shout almost made me drop my camera. Pierce Martinson, with Dr. Kendrick looming behind him, hurried over and dropped to his knees next to Reid's body. He clasped Reid's hand to his chest and glared at the SMTs. "What have you done to him?"

"I'm sorry," Ky said gently. "We pulled him from the water, but we weren't able to resuscitate him. Ewan, our *achubydd*, wasn't able to detect any calon spark at all."

Pierce's jaw worked, his eyes blazing. "Get away from him."

Ky glanced up at Dr. Kendrick's impassive face. "We should really transport him to United Memorial. We'll need to—"

"No! I'll take him. I won't have you desecrating his body. We…we have our own traditions. Our own rituals."

Ky waited for Dr. Kendrick's curt nod before he stood along with the others and backed away. As the Queen's official Champion, Dr. Kendrick is like the SAC for supe law enforcement. If he said Pierce could take the body, then Pierce could take the body.

He handed Pierce a bulky bundle that the older man unfolded and shook with a snap before spreading it on the ground next to Reid. In the lights from the ambulance, it looked blood red and had the kind of texture that I associated with velvet.

The SMTs had already removed Reid's overcoat. Ky stepped forward as if to help move the body onto the—shroud, I guess?—but Pierce barked, "No! He is my son. No one but me shall attend him."

Everyone, including Dr. Kendrick, stepped back respectfully.

For a lean, older guy, Pierce was clearly stronger than he looked, because he gathered Reid's body against him and dead-lifted him onto the shroud as if he weighed no more than a baby. He folded the fabric around him, gently yet precisely, all while murmuring too softly for me to hear. Once Reid was completely wrapped, Pierce stood and made some kind of gesture over the body, which caused Zuri, who was perched on Ky's shoulder, to fluff her neck feathers until Ewan smoothed them with a finger.

Pierce strode over to Reid's sports car. I expected him to crack the trunk, but instead he opened the rear door. He returned to Reid's body and dead-lifted—I really needed to find another word—it again, carrying it with measured tread to the car and arranging it tenderly across the back seat, something I could have sworn was impossible.

Yeah, I really needed to stop being surprised by supe abilities.

After he shut the door, he leaned his head on the car roof and murmured something else. Then he turned to face us. I'm not sure what I expected to see in his expression. Grief? Sure. Anger? Understandable.

What I didn't expect to see was a glimmer of triumph amid the fury.

"I've warned the council. I've warned them multiple times about Lachlan Brodie's instability. And you see the result!"

Dr. Kendrick eased up on his impression of a Stonehenge menhir, although not by much. "We don't know that Mr. Brodie is responsible for this."

Pierce scoffed. "My boy drowned. His fiancé missing. The bastard's boat gone. Of course he's responsible. And I expect the council to do what's right. I expect justice. I expect Brodie form-locked and hunted on the high seas." His upper lip lifted in a sneer. "Although he doesn't deserve even that much of a chance. You ought to unsheathe that useless broadsword of yours, Kendrick, and behead him where he stands."

"Mr. Martinson," Dr. Kendrick said wearily, "we cannot—"

"I'm taking my son home for proper burial." He glared at all of us, although his eyes narrowed when they landed on me. "I expect to hear a satisfactory response from the council. By dawn."

He climbed in the driver's seat and peeled out of the lot like a Formula One racer.

Dr. Kendrick's shoulders slumped and he ran a hand through his hair. "Damn." He glanced at the SMTs. "Thank you for your efforts. You may go now."

They nodded to him and returned to their ambulance. Once they'd left, Dr. Kendrick turned to me. "I believe you've taken photographs?"

"Uh...yeah." I wiped my suddenly damp hands on my jeans. Dr. Kendrick was one of the people who'd strongly objected to my shots when I was still working for the tabloids. Was he about to demand my camera?

But he just heaved a weary sigh. "Good. I'm not looking forward to this trial." A lopsided smile tugged at his lips, and for a moment, despite his almost impossible fae beauty, he looked completely human. "The magicians' faction will take this as justification for their own independent council outside of supe jurisdiction. They've been demanding it for centuries. Please tell my brother I depend on him—on all of you at Quest —to prevent that if you possibly can."

"We'll, um, do our best?"

"I can ask no more. But if you fail..." He gazed out at the moon, about to disappear into the sea. "Well, I suppose we can't expect anything to last forever, can we?"

He strode off across the lot, and it wasn't until he disappeared around the corner that I realized I should have asked him if there was another FTA stop closer than Ted's cave. On the other hand, I couldn't very well leave my Honda here.

I climbed behind the wheel, my thoughts in turmoil and my throat tight. Lachlan was probably a liar and manipulative to boot. But after I'd seen that expression on his face when he'd spoken to Blair, the one so like Ted's, I'd never imagined he could be a cold-blooded murderer.

Shakespeare had it right. *What fools these mortals be*. Or at least what a fool this particular mortal could be when his stupid heart got in the way of his head.

# CHAPTER
# SIXTEEN

I parked the Honda at my place, not even able to scare up annoyance when an entire bushel of brown fir needles whomped onto the hood from apparently nowhere. Dryad spitefulness seemed irrelevant in the face of murder and betrayal.

Shouldering my camera bag, I trudged up the hill toward the cave. Jeez, would this day ever be over? It felt like it had lasted three weeks already. I hoped Zeke would have some of his amazing coffee ready at the office, because I had a feeling the day would get longer before it got shorter.

Below me, the lights of Dewton twinkled like the promise of welcome and comfort. Could I stop in at Wanda's, the 24-hour diner where I ate more meals than I ate at home, for a to-go coffee and some doughnuts? It was tempting—especially since I suspected I'd need to tip my FTA driver with more than gold at this time of night. But the thought of walking down the hill and then back up again was more than I could handle. I'd depend on Zeke. He'd never let us down yet.

I yawned as I slogged into the clearing. Maybe I could catch a nap under one of the conference tables. Maybe I should suggest we convert one of the unused workrooms into a staff lounge with a couple of comfy sofas. But then I remembered the way the hair rose on my neck as I crossed Pierce Martinson's pentagram. *Not a workroom then.* Maybe one of the conference rooms. It's not like we needed all of them. Or maybe I could ask Zeke to requisition a cot for my office.

If I moved my desk into the corner and shoved the—

"Awp!" My startled squawk echoed in the dark woods and a massive hand clamped over my mouth.

"Matthew. It's me."

I froze at Lachlan's distinctive pronunciation of my name. Terror warred with anger in my belly. Terror because this man was a murderer. *Probably* a murderer. Anger because he'd played Quest, played *me* in his little game to get his husband back.

The way my ears started to burn, anger was winning. I think I mentioned that I was a complete idiot where my heart was concerned?

I elbowed Lachlan in the belly. He uttered a muffled *oof*, but I suspected my elbow got the worst of it because *ow*. The man— or rather, the selkie—must have abs of literal steel.

"I'm not going to hurt you, Matthew, but you need to be still. It's not safe."

I made myself go motionless, and after a moment, Lachlan lifted his hand—although not very far. Apparently, he was having some trust issues as well.

"I *know* it's not safe," I hissed, "considering I'm alone in the woods with a murderer."

"What?" He grabbed my shoulders and spun me to face him. "I'm not a murderer." His Rs rolled hard enough to tumble down the hill.

"Tell that to Reid Martinson." I glared at him. "Oh wait. You can't. Because he's dead."

His eyes widened. "Reid's dead?"

I jerked myself out of his hold. "As if you didn't know." I took a step backward. "And before you get any ideas about getting rid of me too to cut down on witnesses, everybody knows."

His eyebrows drew together. "Everybody knows what?"

I sniffed. "Everything."

He reached for me again, but when I stumbled back, the expression on his face could almost be one of hurt. But then psychopaths had to be good actors, right? "Please, Matthew. This is important. Do they suspect about Wyn?"

"You mean that you staged this whole harassment scam in an elaborate ruse to get him back?"

His expression morphed to one of...exasperation? "I didn't— Goddess bless, I don't want him back. If I'd wanted to stay with him, I'd never have filed the sundering petition."

I shoved my hands in my jacket pockets. Where were my FTA tokens? If I could just activate one— *Crap*. They were in my breast pocket. No way I could grab one surreptitiously. "*You* filed it? But Wyn is the one who wanted the split. Why didn't he do it? Is this another lie?"

"What? I've never lied to you." He scrubbed his hands over his face and for the first time, I noticed that he looked exhausted, with dark circles under his eyes visible even in the wan starlight. "Severing the knot... For a supe it's...bad. Especially for fae. For one thing, it means admitting that you've failed, and for some, being tarred as a failure is enough to turn you outcast."

Despite myself, I was interested. "But wouldn't that be true for both—or however many—partners are involved?"

He shook his head. "The one who lodges the request is considered to be surrendering. It's shameful to ask to be released from vows. Wyn and I weren't a good match, but I didn't want him to bear that burden."

"Yet you didn't mind bearing it yourself?"

He shot me a wry glance from under the screen of his hair, and my heart bumped sideways. "I'm as near an outcast as makes no difference already. And I don't care if folks dislike me or disapprove of me. I can handle it. My shoulders are broad."

*I'll say.* But I was beginning to think that just because he was capable of carrying the weight, it didn't mean he should be forced to. "I saw you arguing with Reid earlier. I saw you on the *Cridhe na Mara* with Wyn."

He winced. "Ah, bugger. Did anyone else spot us? Spot Wyn?"

"Not unless Blair did. They're the one who..." I swallowed thickly. "They discovered Reid's body and called me."

Lachlan muttered something under his breath. "They were probably looking to spend the night on the boat. I let them kip there when their father's on a bender." He carded his hands through his hair, but it fell forward again immediately. "Has everyone cleared off now?" I nodded. "I hope this won't keep them from taking shelter then."

"They'll have a little difficulty with that since the boat's gone."

"What?"

I'd expected Lachlan to roar loud enough to be heard in Portland, but that one word was uttered in a broken whisper. Unease writhed in my middle. He couldn't be that good an actor, could he?

He sank to the ground. Or rather his knees seemed to buckle, and he dropped like a boulder with really good hair. "They stole my boat. The bastards stole my boat."

"Everyone assumes you took it out." The combined desolation and anger in Lachlan's expression was like a punch to the throat. "Th-they figure you went all seal-y and took Wyn over the side." I tried to keep my game face on. I'd have to have a good-cop/bad-cop vibe to be an effective investigator, right? Although I probably couldn't even manage cop-with-a-doughnut vibe. "Did you? Take him into the water?"

He shot me an irritated glance. "Of course I didn't. I don't have my skin, do I? And besides, Wyn couldn't survive. He's not my mate anymore, and he's a fresh water bloke. Salt water would do him in."

"That's kind of what they think you did. Him. In, I mean."

He surged to his feet, and this time anger was front and center. "So you think I killed two people? Why in bloody blazes are you standing here talking to me then? Shouldn't you be hauling your sweet arse as far and as fast as you can run?"

There he went again with comments about my ass. Now was not the time to delve into that...as it were. "Are you saying you didn't kill them?"

"No, I bloody well didn't." He stomped across the clearing like a charging bull. I was surprised the ground didn't shake. Or maybe it did, because a few fir needles pattered onto my shoulders. "Wyn showed up with a black eye, all right?"

My eyes widened. "Reid hit him?"

"Aye," Lachlan growled. "And it wasn't the first time. That's why he broke up with Reid to begin with, back before he married me."

"Is that *why* you married him? To keep him safe?"

Lachlan jerked a nod. "Partly. He was looking for a protector, which is probably why he hooked up with Kendrick first, figuring a bloke with his status could keep the Martinsons at bay. Wyn's a sweet man, though. And it wasn't as if I had blokes lining up to court me. I can be a tad prickly, it seems." He sighed. "But even prickly bastards get lonely now and again."

"Was he..." My throat was suddenly thick. "Was he there to get back together with you? To put a stop to the sundering?"

This time Lachlan's expression was exasperated. "No, he wasn't. But wouldn't matter if he was. It became pretty clear we weren't suited. A brackish union, Kendrick called it. An unlikely match, and he wasn't wrong. If I'd stopped to think about that before we tied the knot in the first place, I'd have saved both of us a lot of bother." He shoved his hands in his jacket pockets. "He did ask for my help though."

"What kind of help?" See, I was getting the hang of this interviewing business. It wasn't because I just wanted to keep talking to Lachlan. Nope. Not at all.

"What do you reckon? To get away, of course." He laughed softly. "I should have thought of that the first time, instead of tying him to me so he'd be right where Reid could find him, did he want to look."

"I take it he wanted. To look."

Lachlan lifted an eyebrow. "Looked and found. His fiancé, wasn't he? That's what Pierce bloody Martinson said. Although why he would agree to that..." he said softly.

I wondered the same thing myself. "So he came to you because he knew you'd help him?"

"Aye. We shouldn't be married anymore—it's not doing either one of us any good—but I don't want him to be some rich blighter's punching bag either."

"I doubt Reid'll be doing much punching now," I muttered.

"So he's really dead, then?"

"As a herring. And by the way, there was a fifth dead one nailed to the *Cridhe na Mara*'s stern, so I hope you got Wyn's promise to cease and desist on that little hobby."

Lachlan frowned. "He said he didn't. None except the first."

"Have you ever heard of Occam's Razor? Simplest solution is probably the right one. If you've got one vandal sending you chum love notes, you hardly need to look further for a second or a third."

"But he couldn't have." Lachlan ran both hands through his hair. "He met me in the parking lot and went aboard with me. Left with me too."

It was my turn to lift an eyebrow. "Don't suppose you could have been distracted by his presence and not noticed it?" I tried not to wince. Was that jealousy in my tone?

Another disgusted look. "Aside from me smelling it, I'd have noticed something nailed to my boat."

"But it was there while you were both inside. I saw it. Didn't you smell it when you left?"

Lachlan's forehead creased and his mouth turned down, but more from confusion than anger. I hoped. "No. Are you certain?"

"Absolutely. I took photographs, and they'll be time-stamped to prove it." I crossed my arms over my chest. My hand was closer to my pocket now, so I *might* be able to liberate an FTA token surreptitiously. "So where's Wyn now?"

His gaze slid away from me. *A tell.* "I don't know."

"Really? You don't *know*? You realize if you can't produce a living Wyn, the evidence will point to you...disposing of him?"

Lachlan pressed his lips together in a firm line, his jaw doing a fine impression of granite. "I promised I'd keep him safe. I made that promise when we tied the knot, and I'll not break it now just because we're about to sever it."

"Lachlan—"

"And I really *don't* know where he is. I..." His gaze slid sideways again. "I gave him my truck."

"You gave him your truck," I repeated woodenly.

"Not for good," he said, his tone implying I was an idiot for thinking such a thing. "He'll leave it for me to pick up. After he..."

"After he what?"

He gave me an almost hunted look. "I gave him that token. The one I never used."

"The FTA token?"

"Aye. Told him to use it to disappear for a while. He might be in Faerie, seeing as he's fae, but he never liked it there. He's probably found a nice river somewhere to settle in while he gets his bearings. Decides what he wants to do next." He shook his head. "Wish I *did* know where he was. I could let him know Reid's not..."

"Not a threat, seeing as he's dead?"

He jabbed a long finger at me. "I did *not* kill that bugger. We squawked at one another for a good half hour. Well, he squawked and I let him. But once he realized I wasn't about to let Wyn go with him, he got in that Maserati of his and roared off."

A chill slithered down my spine. "You're saying he left."

"Aye." He scowled at me. "Summat wrong with your ears?"

"His car was there. When Blair found his body."

Lachlan winced. "Ah, the poor mite. They've got enough on their plate."

Clearly Lachlan was more concerned with Blair's potential trauma than with Reid's demise. I wasn't sure I blamed him entirely—I liked Blair better than Reid, too, but Reid was dead. Blair could at least recover with the proper support.

There was no recovering from being dead.

"Lachlan. They're looking for you. If you didn't kill Reid—"

"I didn't!"

"Then maybe the best thing you can do is to turn yourself in. I've, er, experienced the tribunal's truth spells. If you're telling the truth, if you're innocent, that'll come out in court."

He gave me a pitying look. "Sorry, mate, but those spells are only 100% effective on humans. Supes can work around them, with the right attitude, ability, or counterspell. They'd never believe me."

"But if you don't come forward, the only testimony they'll have is from Pierce Martinson. He's got you tried and convicted already. And Lachlan—he wants you form-locked."

He snorted. "That'd be a good trick, seeing as I don't have my skin."

His skin. That wasn't in his pack. That he sent me to find. Which was in the cave at my back. Sans skin.

"That's another thing—"

He grabbed my shoulders again. "You've got to give me time, Matthew. Time to prove it wasn't me."

His hands were warm through my jacket. Firm, but not painful. I got the impression that I could step back and he'd let me go. I gazed into his eyes, so dark, and wished for a little more light so I could read them better.

If I did, if I let him go, I could be sending my career as an investigator down the tubes. Heck, I was still on probation with the council. If letting a suspected murderer go free wasn't a violation, I'm not sure what would count as one. I had a location beacon on my phone, installed at the council's insistence so they could track me at their convenience. But I could activate it from my end too.

And I should. Fire it up and let the supe justice system—such as it was—take it from here.

But the supe justice system had almost mistakenly condemned Ted. It was only Quentin's efforts that saved him. If Lachlan truly was innocent, could I trust the system to get it right this time? He didn't have a Quentin.

All he had was me.

The wind soughing through the firs sent another shower of needles over me. But not over Lachlan. *Freaking dryads.* I took a deep breath.

"Okay, look. I'll let you go. I won't tell anyone I saw you. But you have to promise me something."

His smile nearly lit up the clearing. "Anything."

"You have to promise me that if you can't find any evidence within twenty-four hours—"

"Forty-eight."

"Thirty-six."

"Done."

"In thirty-six hours, you present yourself to the Quest offices and let Mal take you into custody."

He glared at me from under lowered brows. "Does it have to be Kendrick? Can't I give myself up to O'Tierney? Or you?"

I tried not to make too much out of that request. It probably had more to do with Lachlan's antipathy toward Mal than any affection for me. "It's his brother who'll be doing the honors, eventually. But Mal's the one in charge of this case."

"I thought that was you."

*Down, warm fuzzies, down!* "Only temporarily. Besides, I'm a human. Humans have no jurisdiction over supes."

"Most of the time," he muttered, and I remembered the extremely problematic history of human interaction with his species, not to mention our abysmal track record with anyone classed as *other*, even if they were human too.

"Promise."

He looked me in the eye and placed one fist over his heart. "I vow it on the heart of the sea."

I had to assume that was a binding vow. "Okay." I dug my keys out of my pocket. "You won't be able to use the FTA. With the Queen's Champion out looking for you, any driver would take you straight to him or risk...whatever punishment is standard these days." I was pretty sure flogging wasn't on the table anymore, but I couldn't hazard a guess on what had replaced it. I gave Lachlan my address. "You can take my car. Although I'll warn you, I've got a—" The wind blew a cluster of pine needles straight into my mouth.

"Dryads?" Lachlan asked wryly. "Don't worry, lad. They steer clear of salt water folk like me." He took the keys and gave my shoulder a brief squeeze. "Thank you. I'll not forget it."

He disappeared into the trees, and I sighed. I needed to get back to Quest and confess everything to Mal, from letting the prime suspect go all the way back to the break-in—

The break-in. The pack. The absence of skin. "Lachlan!" I ran to the edge of the clearing. "Lachlan!" But he was gone.

"*Crap.*" I retrieved the pack from the cave and called up my FTA driver.

Time to face the music.

# CHAPTER SEVENTEEN

When I got back to the office, every light was on, as if it was the middle of the regular workday instead of approaching three AM. Zeke was sitting at his desk, fingers blurred with the speed of his typing as he peered at his monitor through his bespelled glasses.

Pro tip: That's a sure way to identify demons—they'll always wear glasses. Their eyes were configured for lightless Sheol, so banging around here in the Upper World is impossible without a vision spell, and nobody's figured out how to bespell contacts without making them disintegrate. So if you see someone wearing glasses? Could be a demon. Just saying.

Zeke smiled at me as I trudged through the reception area. "Hello, Hugh." His smile faded. "You look..." He blinked, and then his eyes widened. "Oh, Hugh. What have you done?" He bit his lip. "I'm sorry. I shouldn't have peeked, but you're so tired it just...fell out."

*Crap.* The other thing about demons? It's really hard to keep a secret from them because their *raison d'être* is to make deals with humans for their souls. So guilt, longing, need? Yeah, they can read those just like a freaking tweet. Of course, considering all the stuff I had going on, it was more like a doomscroll.

"Mal in?"

Zeke nodded. "Niall too. There's been a bit of fuss around tonight's events."

Fuss. That was one way to put it. "Should I go in?"

He gave me a pointed look. "You'd better. Before they come to you."

"Right."

"I'll bring coffee."

I shot him a thumbs-up as I trudged past his desk and down the hall toward the bosses' offices. I heard rumbly voices from the one on the right—Mal's—so I knocked on the half-open door and walked in.

They stopped talking at once. I smiled weakly and tossed Lachlan's pack onto the loveseat in the corner, although I was more careful with my camera bag, setting it gently on the glass-topped coffee table with the gnarled wooden base that made it look as if it was growing out of the floor. *Ugh.* Could a dryad possess our coffee table? It didn't bear thinking about.

I turned to face my bosses. "Uh, hi." They stared at me stonily, arms crossed like freaking fae bookends. "So I guess we need to talk about some stuff, huh?"

"You think?" Mal carded his hands through his hair. "When I sent you to interview Wyn, I told you to keep Lachlan away."

Surprise made my breath catch, but the relief that followed released it again. They didn't know about the break-in? About me letting Lachlan go? "Y-you did. I finished documenting the latest vandalism and left while he was selkied up, presumably headed out to sea. I have no idea how he found out where I was going, let alone that he planned to show up."

"You—"

Niall nudged Mal in the side. "That's fair. I'm not sure *you* could have kept him away, boyo, so don't take the piss out of Hugh."

Mal scowled. "All right. Fine. But when he left the Martinsons' place, why didn't you stick with him?"

"I wasn't supposed to tail him. I was supposed to interview Wyn. Besides, he made it pretty clear he didn't want me around.

He's the client." I shrugged. "And I'm human. It's not like I could violate his wishes."

"Also fair," Niall said. "But you must have made some kind of impression on him. It was you he called from St. Stupid's, not Mal or me or even the office."

I blinked. "I assumed he'd tried and didn't get through. He, ah, didn't call you first?"

Niall shook his head. "You were his first thought."

The warm fuzzies were back, although given what I had to confess to my bosses, sheer terror was doing a bang-up job of beating them off with a really big stick. "Oh." I licked my dry lips. "Probably because I'd just spent the afternoon with him and he knew you weren't available."

They exchanged glances and then shrugged at almost the same moment. Mal turned his cobalt gaze on me and I tried not to squirm. "What did you talk to him about in the hospital? Did he give you any information about the attack?"

"Not exactly." I drew out the word. "But he asked me to retrieve something for him. Something that was stolen."

Mal's perfect eyebrows drew together. "Why in blazes did he ask you to do that?"

I glared at him, because this was something that still bugged me about the way the supe community worked. "Maybe because you lot don't have anything like detectives or police. All you've got is…is…" I flung my arms out. "Us. Quest. Since I was the one you fobbed him off with, who else was he going to ask?"

Mal had the grace to flush. "Yeah, sorry about that, mate. Bryce is always on me about how I need to separate my personal feelings from my professional responsibilities."

"Let's face it, Mal." I took a breath because I could almost see a pink slip dancing in front of my eyes. "You didn't think he had a case, did you? You thought it was nothing but a nuisance. That *he* was nothing but a nuisance. So you assigned your least effective employee to babysit him."

"Now hold on there, mate—" Mal said.

"You're not our least effective employee," Niall said at the same time.

"No? Who would that be, then? Zeke?"

Zeke, who'd just walked in with the coffee tray, stumbled to a halt, the spoons clinking and mugs wobbling. "What?"

Niall pinched the bridge of his nose. "We are *not* having this conversation."

Zeke stared at me, wide-eyed. "What conversation?"

"The one where they try to convince me that I'm not here because the council couldn't figure out what else to do with me," I said acidly.

Mal uncrossed his arms and pointed at me. "Now *that* is not true. If you must know, I petitioned to have you work for us."

"We both did," Niall said, a little less testily "The same way we petitioned for Zeke. You're both here because we want you here. You both bring things to Quest that the two of us"—he cast a sardonic glance at Mal—"meatheads that we are, don't. To be honest, the whole notion of Quest Investigations was a way for the King and Queen to put their least law-abiding citizens to work in a way that would keep us out of mischief."

Mal snorted. "Wouldn't put it past their manipulative majesties to have maneuvered us into hiring both of you in the first place. Maybe they reckoned you'd keep us in line. Give us somebody other than ourselves to think about."

Well, that was an interesting take. I hadn't known exactly why Mal and Niall had formed Quest. It was already in place by the time I'd had my little run in with the tribunal. I cleared my throat. "Well, in that case, there's probably more you should know about the, er, events of the day."

Mal took the tray out of Zeke's hands and set it on the coffee table. "In that case, why don't we all settle in with a cuppa and hear all about it."

"What, me too?" Zeke squeaked.

"Couldn't do without you, mate. Although..." Mal retrieved the coffee tray and handed it back to Zeke. "Maybe get us set up in the small conference room. I promised Alun hourly updates. I'll join you after I chat with him."

I rubbed my chest, which had tightened at Mal's words. He and Niall might *say* they trusted us, but Mal clearly didn't want us on the call with Dr. Kendrick. He must have caught something in my expression because his changed from resigned to exasperated.

"I can tell what you're thinking, mate, and no, it's not because you're not trustworthy enough to be in on the call." He winced, gripping his nape with one hand. "But it's not well pleasant getting reamed out by my brother with my entire team listening in, yeah?"

Niall pushed himself off the desk where he'd been perching. "I'm going to the loo." He whisked out of the room as if he had Zeke's demon super speed.

Mal laughed. "Smart man, Niall O'Tierney. He's been given the rough side of Alun's tongue before and isn't keen to repeat the process." He gestured to the door. "Go on. We'll join you presently."

I collected the pack and my bag, but slowly. I didn't feel right about letting Mal bear the brunt of Dr. Kendrick's anger and frustration. Especially when I had information I hadn't disclosed.

"Mal. There are some things you should—"

Mal held up both palms. "Hold it right there, mate."

"But I—"

"Nope." He took my elbow and hustled me toward the door, but let Zeke rattle out ahead of me. "You've had a day, and no mistake. I can tell that much. But I can also tell you're conflicted about whatever it is." His smile was kind, something few people expected of brash Mal Kendrick. "If you tell me about it now, I'll have to pass it along to Alun. I'd rather hear it all first so we can strategize." He chuckled. "An admirable man, my brother, but he has a little trouble with nuance, if you take my meaning. Now go."

I nodded and stooped to gather my bag and Lachlan's pack

"And Hugh?" I turned back, and this time Mal's expression had moved beyond kind and into pitying. "Remember. Brodie's not Ted, mate."

My stomach tumbled. "I know." I lifted my chin. "But he's our client. And we owe him the best job we can do. We owe him the truth."

"Aye." He gripped my shoulder, which was still littered with pine needles. "But you need to be ready if that truth condemns him. We've had a run of luck with our cases so far, but one of these days, one of our clients will be guilty as all the hells. Someone's got to break our winning streak."

I met his gaze steadily for maybe five seconds before I turned away and trudged down the hall, hearing his office door close behind me.

The little conference room at the end of the hall was smaller than either Mal or Niall's office—hence the Little Conference room—although it was bigger than my cubby on the third floor. Before you judge Mal and Niall for being stingy, let me be clear: They'd offered me a larger spot, but after years in newsroom bullpens, a succession of cramped apartments, and my current little house, I felt more comfortable in a smaller space.

Zeke was already arranging the coffee service on the round oak table in the corner where windows looked down over the Pearl District streets. "You know," he said, "this is the same view I used to have from my quarters upstairs."

I jerked my head up to stare at him, which was why I completely missed the credenza and sent Lachlan's pack tumbling to the ground, the damning overcoat bursting out of the still-open zipper. I cursed under my breath as I set my camera bag down. "You lived here? In this building?"

Zeke nodded as he arranged a coffee mug at each place, the handles at precisely four o'clock. "When I worked for Supernatural Selection, under the Sheol work-release program."

"I knew you'd been in the program." I gave up trying to stuff the coat back in the pack and tossed it over the back of one of the extra chairs Zeke had positioned at the table. "But it must have been a little claustrophobic, living at the same place you worked."

Zeke smiled his sweet smile. "It was, a little. I used to stand at the window and dream about being able to go outside."

I stared at him. "Hold on. You were imprisoned in this building?"

He shrugged. "It was better than Sheol." He rolled his eyes. "*Anything* was better than Sheol. It was before Hamish"—his voice made *Hamish* sound like *paradise*—"and there were still rules. So many rules." His smile returned even wider. "It's so much better now."

*Understatement.* Man, if I ever started feeling sorry for myself again, all I had to do was think about what Zeke'd had to endure. Not saying it would make me never whine again, but it certainly put things into perspective.

I made sure to give Zeke the chair with the view out the window. We'd just gotten settled when Mal and Niall walked in. Mal had the expression on his face that he usually only wore when his coffee had gone cold.

Niall, who was never one to let sleeping dogs—or fae—lie, grinned at him. "Good chat with your brother, then?"

"Shut it, O'Tierney," Mal growled as he dropped into a chair. He wrapped his hands around his steaming mug—Zeke's coffee serving skills were truly supernatural—and inhaled, his expression clearing. "Ah. Got some of David's coffee beans again, have you?"

Zeke chuckled. "I'm bypassing the middle man now. I've got a standing order with his Aunt Cassie."

Niall picked up his own mug. "How'd you arrange for the archdruid of the entire region to supply our office with coffee beans?"

Zeke shrugged. "I asked."

Mal eyed the tray, which held the carafe, the cream pitcher, and a bowl full of raw sugar lumps. "Ask for a few scones, next time we're here at the devil's hour."

"Devil's hour?" I took a sip of my own coffee, gearing up for an extremely awkward confession.

"Three AM." Mal glanced at the clock over the credenza and winced. "Although we're past that, too. Bugger. Bryce will not be happy with me."

"Actually," Zeke said, "I have a standing order in with Wonderful Mug. The scones will be here in an hour."

"They deliver at four thirty?"

Zeke doctored his own mug. "They open at five. I just piggy-backed our order on their daily bakery delivery."

Mal blinked. "So that's why we always have pastries on in the morning." He beamed at Zeke. "You are truly a wonder, mate."

Zeke ducked his head, his pale skin blotching with red. He was cute as a button, but his blush wasn't exactly elegant.

"Now, Hugh." Mal's expression sobered. "I understand your interview didn't go as planned."

I winced. "Not entirely. Wyn claimed he was only responsible for the first fish. Lachlan believes him."

"Said so, did he, after he showed up and bolluxed up the interview?"

"Not exactly." I took a huge gulp of coffee, burning my tongue.

"Later, then? At the hospital?"

"Um…"

Mal narrowed his eyes. "Maybe you should tell exactly when you had this little chat with our client, otherwise known as supe enemy number one." He nodded at Zeke. "For the record." Zeke nodded and pulled a tablet from apparently thin air. Maybe he kept it in a dimensional pocket, a Sheol storage specialty. Since the Realm Accords, the C-suite demons were making a killing marketing those spells to other supes, but as a demon himself, Zeke manipulated them naturally.

"I saw him in the woods, by Ted's cave." I dropped my gaze to my mug, but the coffee looked like a huge dark eye, staring back at me accusingly. I pushed it away. "After Pierce Martinson took Reid's body away, and the SMTs drove off and Dr. Kendrick left," I said in a rush.

"Hold on." Niall leaned forward. "Are you saying you spoke to him *after* the murder? He *accosted* you? Bloody hells, Hugh, why didn't you set off the emergency beacon? That's what the bloody thing is for."

"He said he didn't do it!"

"That's what they all say, mate," Mal said. "But fact is, we've got one body in hand and another in the bush. Or ocean, as the case may be."

"He says Wyn isn't dead. He's alive. But he doesn't know where." I swallowed thickly. "He, um, gave Wyn his truck and an FTA voucher so he could get away."

Niall muttered something under his breath, and Mal scrubbed both hands over his face. "Grand. Our only witness is in the wind, not to mention the prime suspect."

"Lachlan promised he'd turn himself in after thirty-six hours."

"And they all say that too! Hugh—"

"He promised. On the heart of the ocean. He doesn't break his promises."

"That's true," Zeke said. "Selkies don't, not when they swear on the ocean. If he said he'd turn himself in, he will."

Mal sighed resignedly. "Well, at least he can't have gone far, not if he gave Wyn his truck. He can hardly jaunt into Faerie, or they'd nab him first thing. Ah, bugger." He winced and pushed out of his chair to pace across the room. "He could slip on his bloody seal skin and be off into the water and we'd never find him."

I screwed up my face and my courage. Time to cop to the break-in. "Actually—"

Mal barked a laugh. "I hope you counted the silver, Zeke."

Zeke glanced from me to Mal. "What? We don't have any silver. Do we? Do I need to count it?"

"Just an expression, mate." Mal gestured to the coat flung across the chair. "Since Ronnie Purl's been here, you can bet that something's gone walkabout if he was left unsupervised for five minutes."

Zeke's brow wrinkled. "Ronnie wasn't here. Why do you think he was?"

Mal jerked his thumb at the coat. "Because that's part of Ronnie's restitution, return of which is keeping him out of nick. That's Casimir Moreau's cashmere coat."

# CHAPTER EIGHTEEN

I stared at the coat as though it could sprout fangs of its own. "*Casimir's* coat. Are you sure?"

Mal lifted an eyebrow. "My own wardrobe might be limited" —understatement: Mal wore leather pants and white T-shirts, almost like a uniform—"but that doesn't mean I don't recognize good stuff when I see it. That's a bespoke coat, and Cas's tailor doesn't make that style for anyone else. Besides..." He picked it up by the collar and thrust it out so we could see the label. "It's got his name embroidered on the label."

My jaw dropped. I'd never even thought to check the label, not that I could have read it in the dark. "B-but...what was Pierce Martinson doing with Casimir's coat?"

Niall frowned. "What's Martinson got to do with anything?"

*Whoops again.* I tugged at my suddenly-too-tight collar. "The thing is, see, when Lachlan was attacked, somebody stole his pack." I pointed at it. "That one."

"Not following," Mal growled.

"When I talked with him in the hospital, he begged me to get it back because it held his skin."

Niall leaned forward, his gaze intense. "Martinson is certainly capable of setting the spell that David detected, the one that injured Brodie. He knew Martinson had it?

"Not exactly. He asked me to search for it." I bristled at their skeptical expressions. "We *are* an investigation firm, you know. And he could scarcely report the theft to the human police."

"No, but he could have said something to my brother."

"Well, he didn't. He asked me."

"But, Hugh," Zeke said, his brow puckered with worry, "you wouldn't know where to look."

I gave them a rather sickly smile. "I, um, may have had help?"

"Hey, everyone!" Jordan bounded into the room, two large bags in his arms. "Scones are here!"

Mal stopped pacing and stared at me. "You didn't."

I spread my palms. "He was there at the hospital and he offered, so…"

Jordan's habitual smile faded. "What did I do?"

I sighed. "You helped me break into the Martinson's mansion and retrieve Lachlan's pack."

"Oh. That." He beamed at everyone. "Yeah. Like I told Hugh, I'm really good at finding things." He held out one of the bags. "Scone, anyone? Lemon poppyseed!"

Niall shook his head and pinched the bridge of his nose. Mal heaved an exasperated breath and collapsed into his chair—after snagging a scone from the bag.

"So what you're saying," Mal said around a mouthful of scone, "is that you two bloody *infants* broke into the house of one of the most powerful fire mages in the country?"

Jordan glanced between Mal and me, his brown eyes wide. "There wasn't anybody there. They left before we went inside." He handed the bags off to Zeke, who started arranging the scones on a plate from the credenza. "Except for the person we heard later. But I don't think that was either one of the Martinsons. *They'd* definitely left. Drove out the gates." He perked up again. "That's how we got inside the fence."

"Not helping, Jordan," I murmured out of the side of my mouth.

He blinked at me. "What? It's not that bad if there's nobody home, right? And the door was open. And they shouldn't have had the pack, anyway."

Mal and Niall exchanged a glance. Niall spread his palms as if he was handing the problem over to Mal. "You're one of his teachers, not me."

"It's my fault," I said. I didn't want Jordan to get in more trouble, and given that I'd let Lachlan escape, my ass was pretty much grass anyway. "I'm the one who asked him to help. I could have aborted the mission at any time." I glared at the coat. "But Lachlan had seemed so desperate to get the skin back."

"Wait," Jordan said, frowning. "You told me to find the *pack*. Not the skin."

We all swiveled to look at him. "You mean you knew the skin wasn't in the pack?"

He chortled—and I'd never heard anyone laugh in a way that I could describe that way. "Duh. No seal fur smell." He blushed. "Besides, Mr. Moreau's coat has been, um, close to Mr. Johnson. My old boss. I could never mistake *his* scent."

"Let me get this straight," Niall said, holding his head as if it were about to explode. "Not only did you know that the skin wasn't in the pack, but that Casimir's coat was in there instead?"

"Well, sure. *Anyone* could have told that." He wrinkled his nose. "Well, almost anyone. Who's a werewolf. Who's spent time near Mr. Moreau and Mr. Johnson." Jordan sighed, a dreamy expression on his face. "He's exactly like Thor."

I rubbed the back of my neck. "I thought he was a vampire."

"Not Mr. Moreau," Jordan said disdainfully. "Mr. Johnson. You should see him holding a sledgehammer. He's—"

"Jordan. I don't think we need to get into that, all right?"

He blushed harder. "Right. Sorry."

"What I want to know," Mal said, snagging another scone from the plate, "is how Casimir's coat got into Lachlan's pack anyway, considering Ronnie was supposed to be returning it tomorrow." He glanced at the clock over the door. "Or rather today." He rubbed his eyes. "Shite, I'm tired. Also how in bloody blazes the pack ended up inside the Martinsons' house in the first place."

"Hidden at the back of a closet," Jordan piped up brightly. His smile faded. "That room was weird, though. It made us really uncomfortable, didn't it, Hugh?"

"Leave me out of this," I said, like that was even a possibility.

Niall lifted an eyebrow. "Don't you think you might have felt uncomfortable because you were burgling a fire mage's house?"

Jordan tilted his head, exactly like a quizzical pup. "No. Why would I?"

"Werewolves," Niall muttered. "No concept of boundaries."

An odd warmth was building in my middle, and I didn't think it was the coffee. If Ronnie Purl had Casimir's coat, then there's no way Lachlan could have stuffed it in the pack before he was mugged.

Which meant he didn't lie to me.

Through the haze of fatigue and highly inappropriate elation, I remembered something. "Ronnie Purl was at the Martinsons' place when I went there to interview Wyn. He was working off his community service with the gardeners."

Mal dusted scone crumbs off his fingers. "Well, Your Highness, I think we need to have a little chat with Mr. Purl. What do you say?"

Niall shook his head sadly. "It's so early. It would be a shame to wake him up." Then he bared his teeth in a manic grin. "Let's go get him."

The two of them jetted out of the office like the Cwn Annwn were on their tail.

Jordan sidled over to me as Zeke straightened the coffee tray and repaired Mal's depredations on the scone platter. "Are they mad at me?"

I patted his shoulder. "If they're mad at anyone, it's me, so don't worry." When he continued to bite his lip, I scared up a reassuring smile. "And, Jordan? In case I didn't say it before? Thank you for your help."

Like magic, his expression cleared and he was back to his usual sunny self. "Sure thing, Hugh! Anytime!" He bounced out, as irrepressible as ever.

I shared an amused glance with Zeke. "Is he ever in a bad mood?"

"Not that I've seen." He picked up the coffee service tray. "I don't know how long it will take Mal and Niall to, er, apprehend Ronnie, since if he's shifted, he'll be hard to catch. Will you be heading home in the meantime?" He lifted one shoulder in a half shrug. "Because if you don't mind my saying so, Hugh, you look like you could use a little sleep."

I shook my head. "A *little* sleep probably won't help. Besides, between coffee and residual adrenaline"—not to mention the heavy weight of worry over holding on to my job—"I'll be awake for hours. I might as well stay here and get some work done." I didn't want to miss Ronnie's interrogation, either.

Zeke nodded. "I'll be at my desk. Just let me know if you need anything."

I plodded upstairs to my office, and with every step, *he didn't lie* echoed in my brain. Lachlan hadn't lied to me. I was right to trust him. Of course that didn't mean I hadn't screwed up by A) pulling Jordan into the investigation, B) breaking into the Martinsons', and C) letting Lachlan go with nothing more than a promise.

But hey, one out of a billion ain't bad.

I retrieved my camera from my bag and settled at my desk to download everything from my memory card onto the Quest server. And before you ask—our cloud storage is super secure, since it's located in its own Sheol-brand pocket dimension.

Although the photos rendered onto my screen more rapidly than they had back in the day when I was still freelancing and using a cranky laptop nearly a decade out of date, I was in that weird exhausted state where time seems to stand still.

The shots popped up in chronological order, seeming to float an inch in front of my monitor. I winced when I realized the first ones were from the Great Dryad Debacle. I'd had the shutter release set in continuous mode when Jordan shifted, so I had ample evidence of my own failure to keep a civilian out of Quest business—even a civilian as determined to stick his nose everywhere and "help" as Jordan.

Yep. There he was, peeing on the madrone. And holy crap, those angry dryads were freaky, nearly as freaky as the Martinson's maid, Eleri, blocking the doorway by— *Wait a sec.*

I enlarged one of the first boring shots of the client's identified target, the tree of heaven, that Jordan declared to be the wrong tree. Eleri's, er, foliage had looked one heck of a lot like the tree's compound leaves, with leaflet pairs marching along a central reddish brown stem. Granted, the tree of heaven didn't have thorns, but from what Bryce MacLeod had told me, dryads could manifest more than one plant species if they wanted—and if, presumably, they didn't mind cheating on their tree.

I squinted at my monitor from my rather blurry eyes. One of the dryads in the pack charging behind Jordan—not the first or even the second, but the third—looked an awful lot like Eleri. On the other hand, all of them had started to get that attenuated *twiggy* look, so they looked a lot more like each other than they looked like individuals. A forest rather than distinct trees.

I sent all of those shots into the folder for the dryad case and concentrated on the next set. When Lachlan and I had arrived at his boat, I'd taken long shots of the marina from the edge of the parking lot. It was part of my process—start with the ten thousand foot view and zoom in to the specifics later. Detail shots were important, but without the context of the entire scene, you could miss something important.

I compared that shot to the one from later that night when I arrived to return Lachlan's pack and found him cozied up with

Wyn. His truck was in the same spot as it had been that morning—Lachlan was apparently a creature of habit.

When the shots of Lachlan and Reid facing off rendered, I shifted uneasily. I'd captured evidence of their confrontation in full digital color. Reid's expression was twisted, his mouth gaping with his shouts. Lachlan's brow was thunderous and he looked about as moveable as Haystack Rock. I'd caught one of Wyn, too, peering out of the cabin window, his big dark eyes wide and frightened. But of whom? Bracketed as the shot was by Lachlan's truck and Reid's Maserati, I couldn't tell who he was staring at with that expression of absolute terror.

According to Lachlan, Wyn was trying to escape from Reid. But with Lachlan blocking access—either on or off the boat—maybe he was looking for a way to escape from *Lachlan*. I glanced over my shoulder, as if somebody might be standing in the corner of my cramped office and ask me why I was photographing the argument rather than assisting my client. Old habits die hard, I guess.

The shots from later on, after Reid's body was discovered, were even more cringe-worthy. Lachlan's boat and truck missing, the ambulance lights casting peculiar shadows over the scene, Ky and Pete working futilely over Reid. I'd screwed up the angle on that one, the Maserati blocking Reid's body from the hips down.

I peered at the picture more closely. Something about that car... I pulled up the earlier shot of the argument and compared the two side by side.

Reid's car was in a different spot.

Lachlan had told the truth. Reid *had* left after the argument. The question was, why did he come back? And was Lachlan waiting for him when he did?

# CHAPTER NINETEEN

Zeke poked his head into my office. "Mal's back with Ronnie. He'd like us both to observe."

I glanced at the monitor. I really wanted to see whether I could find additional photographic evidence to support Lachlan's claims, but since my ambition was to climb out of surveillance mode, I locked the screen and followed Zeke back to the Little Conference Room.

Mal was there along with a cringing Ronnie Purl, who looked much more disreputable in his faded Wranglers and rumpled flannel shirt than he had in the gardener's uniform of green polo and chinos. He was clutching a rucksack that looked like army surplus from about the 1950s. His gaze darted from Mal to Zeke to me.

"Niall not joining us?" I asked.

"Nah," Mal said. "Business with his brother." He grinned evilly at Ronnie. "You know the bloke. Tall. Wears a crown. Friend of the elder god who runs the underworld forge."

"All you big supes are the same," Ronnie said sullenly. "It's do this, Ronnie. Don't do that, Ronnie. Toe the line, Ronnie, or it's off to the forge with you." He bared his teeth. "Last time I was here, you *promised*. You said it would all be okay, long as I gave the stuff back and showed up for that stupid community service."

Mal leaned against the table, ankles and arms crossed. "You buggered that, though, didn't you Ronnie, my lad? You *didn't* give everything back."

"No point, was there? He had me by the short and curlies. Said he'd never agreed to the deal. Said I was going to the forge for the rest of my natural unless I did a job for him."

Beside me, Zeke sucked in a breath. I tensed, and even Mal stopped looking so relaxed. "What job?"

"Said it would be easy." Ronnie snorted. "Just pop up to the end of the street and grab a backpack from behind a bunch of trees. 'Cept when I get there, the backpack's not the only thing lying around. That big guy, the selkie, he's laid out like a dead mackerel."

"Didn't you think to help him?" Mal's tone didn't bode well for Ronnie. "Check to see if he was breathing?"

"Oh, he was breathing all right. Like a bellows. But I had my orders, see?"

"Ronnie, you know it's the responsibility of every supe to watch out for the community."

He glared at Mal. "Tell that to Martinson."

"Martinson?" Mal stood up. "Reid Martinson threatened you?"

"Nah. Not him. The other one. His dad. Standing there like butter wouldn't melt in his mouth. He wasn't looking out for me, was he?" His grip tightened on his rucksack strap. "Him with his threats, tossing a ball of fire in his hand like he was flipping a coin."

"Let me get this straight," Mal said. "Pierce Martinson threatened you with imprisonment if you didn't steal Lachlan Brodie's backpack?"

"That's what I said, isn't it?"

"But you'd already returned what you took from him. He had nothing on you."

Ronnie scoffed. "You think a rich dude like him can't plant something on a little guy like me? I'm a ferret shifter. Who'll believe I didn't take whatever it was he'd say I took? I figured my only chance was to do what he wanted."

"But Ronnie," I said, "once you stole the pack, he'd have a hold on you, anyway."

Ronnie's shoulders sagged. "I know." His gaze darted between us again, a sly gleam in his eyes. "So I decided to do things my own way. I snagged the pack, all right, but once I was down the road a piece, I called the SMTs." He shot a defiant glance at Mal. "I knew *I* couldn't help the selkie, but I didn't want to leave him there on his own. I may be a thief, but I'm not a monster."

Mal nodded. "Glad to hear it. That'll speak well for you when this is laid out for the tribunal."

Ronnie peered up at Mal imploringly. "Can't we keep it between ourselves again? Another deal? More community service?" He wrinkled his nose. "No more gardening, though, at least not at Martinson's house. Those effing plants fight back!"

"Give over, Ronnie." Despite his earlier enthusiasm for hauling Ronnie in, Mal's tone was defeated. "That's the only way I can help you."

He sighed. "Guess you'll want this then." He dropped the rucksack to the floor at his feet and unbuckled its straps. He flipped open the top flap and drew out...

Lachlan's seal skin.

"Holy crap," I muttered. "*You* had Lachlan's skin all the time?"

"Not all the time." Ronnie gave the short, smooth fur one last stroke and then handed it over to Mal, although he seemed oddly reluctant to let it go. "I wanted to know what was in the pack that Martinson was so keen on. And this...well, I had Moreau's coat ready to turn over to you, but this was so much nicer. So much softer. So—"

"We get it. You couldn't resist. So you swapped the skin for the coat? Didn't you figure Martinson would notice?"

"I didn't figure he'd care about that. Rich dudes never think they have enough money, do they? Thought he was after the jewels."

Mal and I shared a dumbfounded look. I strode over to the credenza and grabbed the pack. I'd noticed those lumps when it had been bouncing painfully on my back and legs, and wondered why Lachlan would be carrying rocks around. I unzipped the lumpy front pocket and got an eyeful of bling— diamonds, rubies, emeralds, sapphires, all of it jumbled in the pack as if it held no more value than a Crackerjack prize.

"Holy crap," I repeated. I held the pocket open so Mal and Zeke could see.

Mal glanced from the stones to Ronnie, who was ignoring the sparkling mass and gazing longingly at Lachlan's skin. "You weren't tempted to pocket a few of those for your trouble?"

Ronnie gave him a scornful look. "Sparkly stuff isn't my jam. Besides, I figured that's what Martinson wanted. He wouldn't notice one soft thing replaced with another. Besides, the way him and his son rock the black overcoats themselves, I figured they'd be grateful for the addition."

"You were supposed to return that to Mr. Moreau."

A blush painted Ronnie's thin face an unbecoming red. "Oh. Right. Guess that would be a problem, huh?" He brightened. "But since you've got the pack now, you must have the coat too. So we're square. Right?"

"That's as may be," Mal said sternly. "Didn't Martinson check the contents when you turned the pack over to him?"

"Didn't give it to *him*." Ronnie rolled his eyes. "Guys like me don't go to the front door and speak to the lord and master. I went 'round the back to the *tradesman's* entrance and handed it off to that maid of theirs. Then I took off as fast as I could."

Mal scrubbed his hands over his face. "Gwydion's bollocks, what a turn up. Ronnie, go straight to your brother's place and try to stay out of trouble for the next little while. We'll be in touch. Zeke, if you could see him out?"

Zeke held the door open and with one last wistful glance at Lachlan's seal skin, Ronnie scuttled into the corridor.

Mal stared at the empty doorway ruminatively. "What are the chances Martinson was just being a good Samaritan and collecting Lachlan's pack before it could be stolen?"

"Not likely," I muttered, "not the way he was calling for Lachlan's head on a pike. Or rather a harpoon."

Mal shook his head. "Alun said that didn't happen until after he discovered Reid's body."

"So why would he want Lachlan's skin beforehand? At the point he sent Ronnie after the pack, they had everything they wanted: Wyn engaged to Reid, Lachlan agreeing to the sundering, Wyn shacked up at the mansion. It was almost like they were trying to cut off Lachlan's escape route before anybody—including Lachlan—even knew he needed one."

"Not to mention he'd need to know that Lachlan was out cold in the first place, which he couldn't."

"Unless he was responsible." My excitement was rising, despite my exhaustion. "David said Lachlan's injuries were magically induced, not resulting from external trauma."

"That kind of spell..." Mal gripped the back of his neck again. "It's not strictly legal."

"Not *strictly* legal? It shouldn't be *any* kind of legal. Weaponized magic that the mage doesn't even need to be present to invoke? For God's sake, Mal, that's...that's..."

"I know, all right? That's why the council wants to rein in the mages." His jaw firmed, his eyes narrowing. "I think it's time we had a little chat with Pierce Martinson, don't you?"

I winced. "Right now? His son just died. We can't just show up on his doorstep, can we?"

"Considering his actions may have resulted in his son's death in the first place, I'm not inclined to give him any more time to cover his tracks. However, I'll need some time to get dispensation from the council to approach him." Mal retreated behind his desk and unlocked the special compartment where he kept his broadsword. "The negotiations with the mages are at a critical point, and Martinson is one of their primary advocates. We can't give them any excuse for claiming our lot don't take their concerns seriously." He peered at me. "You all right, mate?"

I realized I was squinting at him in an attempt to focus my blurry vision. I blinked, my eyes gritty. "Fine." But the notion that Lachlan was out there, possibly still a target of Martinson— who didn't even have to be there to strike at him—made me chafe at the delay. "Are you sure we have to wait?"

"I'm sure." He gripped my shoulder. "Get some sleep, mate. Be ready to move by full dark."

"I need to tell you. My photographs—"

"Later, mate." Mal's grip tightened. "We'll get it all sorted later. But our priority should be stopping Martinson before he can push through an irreversible punitive action against Lachlan."

I blinked. "But if the judgment is wrong because the charges are bogus, can't the tribunal rescind their ruling? Drop the charges?"

Mal's glance was pitying. "You're talking about supes, mate. Not many of us are *ever* willing to admit we've been wrong, and the higher up you go, the less likely you'll get any mea culpas. Lachlan's best shot right now is to make sure that Martinson never gets a chance to make his case." He let go of me and strode out.

"That's not right," I murmured brokenly, something swirling uncomfortably in my middle. I'd dreamed of magic, of the supernatural, of wonder since I was a boy. Finding out it was real had been a dream come true.

But any fluffy cloud can have lightning in its heart.

And any dream can turn into a nightmare.

I was certain I wouldn't be able to sleep a wink. When I curled up on the loveseat in Mal's office, though, with one hand on Lachlan's seal skin, I was out before I could count to one one thous—

# CHAPTER TWENTY

That night, right after full dark, I stood with Mal outside the Martinsons' closed gates, swamped by a little too much deja vu. There were differences of course, chief among them the giant wreaths of black roses on each arm of the gates and on the front door of the mansion. I glanced sidelong at Mal. While Jordan wasn't bouncing nearby, itching for adventure, the wicked smile on Mal's face was nearly as alarming.

"You're sure the council believed us?" I asked for about the fifth time since Mal had returned to the office, the parchment with the official decree rolled in his hand.

"Enough to delay Martinson's demand for Lachlan's trial in absentia." He flicked the decree with one finger. "This'll keep him busy for a while, justifying his blackmail attempt on poor old Ronnie."

I had my doubts about that. Ronnie was right—money could buy a lot, and I doubted the supernatural community was any more immune to corruption than the human world. Given Wyn's experience with domestic abuse at Reid's hands, there were quite a lot of unfortunate parallels. My rose-colored notion of a wondrous magical world populated by fairies and unicorns was getting more tarnished by the day.

Supes, it seemed, weren't all that different from humans: just as prone to be selfish, greedy, and unscrupulous. They simply had additional tools at their disposal to achieve their ends.

Mal sauntered over to the security pad and pressed the intercom button.

"Who is there?" The speaker was female, so unless the Martinsons had additional staff lurking around, it was probably Eleri, the thorny maid.

"Mal Kendrick, here to see Pierce Martinson."

"I'm sorry, but Mr. Martinson is in seclusion, mourning the tragic death of his son."

"I understand," Mal said, not sounding the least sympathetic. "However, this cannot wait. I have a decree from the supe high council that requires his immediate attention."

"One moment."

Mal winked. "That'll toss a few logs on his fire."

"If you say so," I muttered. I rubbed the back of my head. I was pretty sure my headache had more to do with too much coffee and not enough sleep, but if Pierce could lob magical mickeys like baseballs, who's to say he couldn't target Mal or me?

Mal shot me an amused glance. "I know what you're thinking, mate. Offensive magic takes preparation. And the SMA is keeping a lookout."

"SMA?"

"Supernatural Monitoring Agency. Run by sphinxes. Buggers never sleep. If they detect any sketchy weaponized magic at this location, my brother will be here quicker than you can say Bob's your uncle."

"Assuming the SMA hasn't been compromised," I retorted. Mal's eyes widened, and he seemed honestly surprised. "What, you assume they're incorruptible?"

"They're sphinxes!"

"And I seem to remember some jerk claiming that being an angel made anything he did okay, so maybe a little skepticism might be a good thing."

"So you're saying…"

"Watch your back, Mal."

He grimaced. "Bloody hell. Wish I'd brought Niall with me after all."

"Hey! I'm decent backup." I tapped my jacket pocket. "Emergency beacon ready to engage. Zeke stocked me up on FTA tokens for a quick—" A clump of fir needles plopped onto my head. I brushed them away. "*Argh!* Lousy dryads."

Mal smirked at me. "I don't doubt your good intentions, mate, dryad feud aside. But you've been inside Martinson's house. Inside his *workroom* without his permission. That makes you vulnerable to him and"—his expression turned apologetic —"a liability to our mission. You'll have to stay outside."

A vine snaked across the ground toward my foot and I dodged to the other side of Mal. "Great. Out here. With the plants."

"Stay in the middle of the lawn and you should be grand. No trees to dump on you. No vines to bind you. Pretty sure grass can't do much damage."

I peered through the gates. Despite how closely the gardeners had shaved the lawn and how aggressively they'd trimmed the hedges, everything was looking decidedly shaggy. Hadn't Ronnie said that the plants fought back? "Somehow that doesn't make me feel any better."

"Relax. The dryads are just throwing a little tantrum. They'll settle down soon enough or…" He leaned over and directed his words to the vine. "I'll have a word with Bryce." The vine curled in on itself and disappeared beneath the bushes. He clapped me on the shoulder. "There you go. You should be fine now."

"Great," I muttered, just as the gates swung open.

Mal grinned at me. "Looks like Martinson's accepting what's good for him." He pointed toward the center of the lawn. "Wait for me there."

"Are you sure?"

"I was the Queen's bloody Enforcer for two hundred years, mate. Trust me. I can take care of myself."

I had to be content with that. I took my place on the lawn, well away from the hedges which rustled rather menacingly—unless that was just the chill breeze that had suddenly kicked up. When the front door opened, a long rectangle of golden light fell over the steps and driveway, casting Mal's shadow halfway to the fence. When the door shut behind him, it was ridiculously dark. All the drapes in the mansion were pulled tight, not a bit of light leaking through, and the lights lining the driveway suddenly winked out.

"Wonderful," I muttered, wrapping my arms across my chest. The lights must be motion sensitive, and with the moon still behind the treetops, unless I wanted to dance the conga across the lawn, I had to make do with starlight.

I wished for one of my night vision camera lenses, or for Zeke's ability to see in the dark. Hmmm... There was a thought. If they made glasses for demons like Zeke or AJ so they could see in the sunlight, could they make the reverse for me? Like night vision goggles only without the funky green outlines? Maybe if I—

A footstep sounded on stone from the other side of the house. *Wait.* If somebody had walked out onto the patio, why hadn't the lights come back on? I squinted through the dark, trying to make out something, anything. Was the darkness next to the house somehow *more* dark? Was it moving?

I listened hard. Could it be more dryad shrubbery shenanigans? It didn't sound like leaves rustling. It sounded like...

The moon peeked over the trees, bathing the grounds in wan light, and I could finally see. But what I could see made no sense whatsoever.

Because the person advancing toward me across the lawn, barefoot and wearing black trousers and a black turtleneck, was Reid Martinson.

# CHAPTER
# TWENTY-ONE

"Y-you're dead," I croaked.

Reid's smirk wasn't nearly as engaging as Mal's. In fact, it raised the hair on my neck. "Death," he drawled. "Such a relative state, don't you agree?"

I backed away, trying to keep a safe distance between us. Although I wasn't entirely sure what constituted a safe distance from somebody who was recently extremely waterlogged and not breathing. "It's always seemed pretty final to me."

He wagged a finger almost playfully. "Ah, that's because you're mired in those limited human perceptions. So one dimensional." He shook his head pityingly. "It's sad, really. If you only knew..."

"Knew what? That you're an entitled, abusive SOB whose father's been throwing money at him all his life to compensate for him being essentially...what is it now?" I tapped my chin, trying for a little bravado. "Oh, yes. *Human.*"

That ripped away Reid's mischievous veneer. "I'm *not* human," he snarled. "I never was. But now I'm so much more than you could ever aspire to."

"What? You mean recently deceased?"

He advanced on me. "I mean extraordinary. Powerful. *Invincible.* Not even death can stop me."

I tried to cover my stumbling retreat with bravado. "Please tell me you're not going to break out with a *bwahahaha.*"

Instead of making him angry, though, my pathetic little snark seemed to settle him. I took advantage of his relative calm to sneak my hand toward my pocket and the emergency beacon.

"Ah ah ah," he said, which was a little too close to *bwahahaha* for my liking. "None of that." He flicked a finger at me and something jerked against my hip. "I think you'll find that your little beacon is...how did you put it? Recently deceased."

I shoved my hand into my pocket and pulled out the device, although I had to drop it because it was *hot*. It fell to the grass, smoking, all its LED indicators extinguished. "How did you—"

"Death. It's what I do now." He paused as if a thought had just occurred to him. "No. Not what I do." He grinned, and in the moonlight, he looked more like a skull than a man. "Who I *am*."

My knees threatened to buckle and my fingers went numb. "Necromancer," I whispered.

"Exactly!" His grin widened. He looked positively delighted. Or positively deranged. "The only one in existence now. So that makes me *extra* special." His delight morphed into menace. "That makes me a god."

"That makes you a criminal." And probably a psychopath. "Necromancy is illegal!"

"Shortsighted, hide-bound thinking," he scoffed. "The last refuge of the weak, those without the courage and *strrrength*"—he accompanied his rolled Rs with a raised fist—"to complete the rituals."

The numbness in my fingers had reached my heart. "What rituals?"

He strolled toward me and I noticed that where he stepped, the grass withered. "Little deaths. Insignificant, really."

"Except to whatever died."

He scoffed. "Fish. They're hardly worth noting."

My jaw sagged as the pieces fell into place. "It was you. *You* put the dead herrings on Lachlan's boat." I retreated further, almost to the hedge and its aggressive vines, but given a choice between surly dryads and a megalomaniacal psychopath whose touch was literally death? No brainer.

"Not the first one." In the moonlight, his skin was dead white. "But it didn't take much to convince Wyn to take that step after the dead thing washed ashore. Not when we'd made sure he'd been rendered...suggestible."

Suggestible? "You roofied him?"

He waved a negligent hand. "Drugs are so crude. Spells are more elegant."

"So you *magically* roofied him. Is that how you got him to cheat on Lachlan in the first place?"

"That oaf. Wyn would have left eventually. We merely... accelerated the process." His expression darkened. "Then the little fool got cold feet after I had him call the next herrings to me. He actually had the audacity to leave me. Me!"

"Yeah," I muttered. "Go figure." The hedge was brushing my back now, and I could swear that its leaves were quivering. Trying to decide how best to throttle me? Frankly, I didn't really care. "Still not getting why you're standing here instead of six feet under."

"So ignorant, you humans. Never see what's right in front of you. Once I'm in charge, that will change. You'll be much easier to control once you understand exactly where you fall on the food chain." He spread his arms wide. "Didn't you know? After the little deaths to prepare the vessel—"

"Vessel? As in a boat?" Is that why he'd targeted the *Cridhe na Mara*?

"Can you really be this stupid? *Vessel* as in *receptacle*." He bared his teeth. "The receptacle of power. But before the ascension, before the vessel is *consumed*, those who walk The Path"—I could hear the capitalization in his tone—"must pass the Great Trial to prove ourselves worthy." He stooped and uprooted a blade of grass with a vicious yank. "Most are too weak, too irresolute, too soft to take that step. But I am not weak, irresolute, or soft."

"The Great Trial," I said, my throat dry. Why the heck wasn't Mal coming out? "I take it that means death."

He chuckled. "Maybe you're not so stupid after all. You could make a decent minion under my new order." He tossed the blade of grass aside. It was brown and withered. "And if you're unsatisfactory, you'll do for spell fodder."

"Yeah, sorry if I'm not signing up for that." I was practically sitting inside the hedge by now.

"Nonsense. You'll be so grateful to set aside burdens not meant for your frail shoulders, to take your proper place, that you'll fall on your knees to thank me." He smiled, the most horrifying thing I'd ever seen. "Of course, you'll be on your knees, anyway. And once I've consumed my vessel—"

"Hold on. I thought you'd already done that."

He scowled. "No. The Great Trial first. *Then* the sacrifice of the vessel."

Holy crap. Was he intending to murder Wyn for this ascension of his? No wonder the poor guy turned to Lachlan for help. "If Wyn was your vessel, that'll be a little tough, considering he's disappeared."

If I thought that last smile was horrifying, it had nothing on his grin. "Wyn? He was the conduit. The connection. The…" He laughed, and it was totally a *bwahahaha*. "The *bait* to lure the proper vessel to me at the proper time."

My knees finally gave out, and only the sturdy hedge kept me from falling on my butt. "You're not… You don't mean…"

"You?" He laughed. "Human blood isn't potent enough to exalt me."

The shoe dropped, and my stomach threatened to rebel all over Reid's bare toes. "Lachlan. You've targeted him from the first."

Reid sighed, almost dreamily. "The raw *potential*. You've no idea. A king who refuses to take his throne. A supe who lives as human. Who *panders* to humans. All of it is wasted on Brodie. I can make much better use of it. Once I've consumed his essence, I'll achieve my true power."

If this was him on low-power setting, I really didn't want to see what he was like cranked up to eleven.

*Come on, Mal. Now would be a really good time to show up.* "I don't think—"

"Martinson!" The roar from the gates made me lose my balance and fall all the way into the shrubbery.

"Oh, God, Lachlan, not *now*." I struggled to regain my feet, expecting the plants to hinder me, but instead it was almost as if a firm hand—in this case, a branch—pushed me upright. "Get back, you idiot," I shouted.

Naturally, he didn't listen. He came charging across the driveway and onto the lawn like an avenging angel. Okay, so the angels I knew weren't exactly the avenging type, but you get the idea. He was big and built and really, really pissed off.

I'd never seen anybody as beautiful.

*God damn it.*

Reid's expression turned absolutely avaricious. Mine probably wasn't all that different—although for a different reason—but mine was also infused with a healthy dollop of terror. How exactly was Reid planning to *consume* Lachlan? Did he need to touch him the way he touched the grass? Could he point his finger at Lachlan and just *zap* him like he'd done to my beacon? Clearly, I needed to brush up on necromancy lore.

Assuming I got out of this alive.

Lachlan stopped a good fifteen feet from Reid, and I was surprised Reid didn't burst into flames from the force of his glare. "Where's my skin, you bloody bastard?"

"Don't worry," Reid said. "We have it safe inside. You'll get it in good time."

I blinked. He didn't know Jordan and I had taken the pack? Unless...

My belly clenched tighter. Oh, God, could he have broken into the Quest offices? Stolen the skin? Hurt Zeke? Demons were especially susceptible to necromancy, and if this jerk had harmed him… Only one way to find out.

"We know you paid Ronnie Purl to steal Lachlan's backpack," I called.

He shot me an irritated glance. "We shouldn't have had to pay him at all, considering he owed *us* for having the temerity to steal from us in the first place. It hardly matters how we acquired it though. The point is that we've got it. And once the council rules to form-lock Brodie, nobody will care how."

So he didn't know the skin was gone. Good. Guess necromancy didn't make you omnipotent and all-knowing, despite Reid's delusions of godhood.

He turned back to Lachlan. But Lachlan wasn't paying attention to him. He was looking at me. "You all right, lad?"

"Fine. But you need to— Look out!"

Lachlan dove to one side in a shoulder roll and fetched up in a crouch at the base of the hedge. Consequently, the energy blast from Reid's outthrust hand missed him and hit a rose bush. Its leaves immediately withered and browned, its blooms blackening.

Behind me, the hedge thrashed and rattled. I started to grin. *Oh, buddy, you just made a big mistake.* For the first time since the Great Dryad Debacle, I was thankful for my stalkers.

As Reid advanced on Lachlan, I turned to the shrubs and said, "Go get him!"

The words had barely left my mouth when vines shot out from under the hedge, bypassing me and Lachlan completely, twining around Reid's ankles and up his legs. Reid glanced down, annoyed rather than terrified as I would have been, and flicked them with his fingers. Some of the leaves died and fell off, but other tendrils took their place. Soon he was tearing at the vines with both hands. But as the vines crept up to his hips, fewer leaves falling by the second, he was clearly losing the battle. Without his full power, without consuming his *vessel*, he apparently didn't have enough juice.

Unfortunately, he figured that out at the same time as I did. His head jerked up, and he focused on Lachlan.

"I was going to do this in the sea, to prove my dominion over the water. But unlike my late unlamented father"—*wait, what?* —"I'm willing to abandon elegance for expediency."

"Your father's dead?" I croaked.

He shrugged. "He will be. I don't need him anymore, now that he's performed the resurrection ritual. Besides, he had some preposterous notion that I would be subservient to him as the elder mage." He scoffed. "As if."

"So you *consumed* him too?"

His face twisted. "Of course not. That's revolting. He was my *father*. I've arranged a more suitable end for him. Neither fire nor man can last very long in a room without air, and I was able to cut a pretty sweet deal with the air mage who'd been snapping at his heels, looking for dominance rather than cooperation." He reached into a sheath at his belt and drew out a dagger as long as my forearm. "I'll deal with her later. If she's not willing to submit to my rule..." He brandished the knife, admiring the flash of moonlight on the blade.

If Reid had trapped his father in an airless room and Pierce was with Mal at the time... I needed to get into that house. At least with Reid immobilized, the vines holding him in place, I might have a chance.

But Lachlan—that *idiot*—walked toward Reid as if he was offering himself on a platter.

"Lachlan, for God's sake, stay *away* from him."

"He must learn to stop preying on the less privileged and powerful." He strode closer. "He doesn't scare me."

"Well, he should! He's a freaking necromancer, and you're his chosen freaking *vessel*. He kills you and we'll *all* be less privileged and powerful. Except you. You'll be dead."

For a wonder, Lachlan actually stopped. He looked at me, a grin splitting his face. "Ah, lad. What makes you think I'd let him win?"

"But Mal's inside. He might be trapped. Dying. If we—" A figure appeared from around the side of the house. My initial relief morphed into alarm, because it wasn't Mal as I'd hoped. No, it was Eleri. If she got up to the same tricks as before, she could immobilize Lachlan—making him a sitting duck—and me, too, leaving me helpless to rescue Mal.

As she raised her hands, I yanked the FTA tokens out of my pocket. I pressed the rune on the top one. "Cludo!" I shouted and cast it aside to activate the next one. "Cludo!" and the next, "Cludo!" And the next. "Cludo!"

Suddenly the lawn was crowded with FTA drivers: a bauchan, a trow, a dryad—wonderful—and Frang, my regular duergar driver. They all looked around quizzically. Frang lifted his heavy brows. "Where to?"

"The house!"

He glanced at it. "You don't need a driver for that. Just walk in."

"No, I don't want to go inside." Well, I did, but I was probably the least qualified to perform a rescue. Duergar, on the other hand, were practically indestructible. "Mal's in there. Possibly trapped in some airless space. I need you to get him out of there. All of you."

"Right," he said. He gestured to the others. "You lot, with me."

The bauchan raced to the door, quicker than the trow and the duergar, but they lumbered after him. The dryad, however, stared from me to Eleri and raised her hands.

"Oh, crap," I muttered, and clenched my eyes shut.

But instead of the onslaught of twigs, branches, and thorns, there was...nothing. Well, nothing except a strangled cry that was abruptly cut off.

When I cracked one eye open, Lachlan was unharmed, but Reid had disappeared inside a veritable straightjacket of twined branches. Only his eyes were visible from inside the plant cocoon. Well, his eyes and the hand holding the knife. As I watched, a thorned tendril snaked around his wrist and insinuated itself between his fingers. The dagger dropped to the grass, accompanied by a spatter of blood.

Lachlan and I gazed at each other, wide-eyed.

"Finally," Eleri said. "I've wanted to do that for *months*." She glanced from the other dryad to me to Lachlan. "Now. Who wants ice cream?"

# CHAPTER
# TWENTY-TWO

If anyone ever asks you whether you want to sit in on a supe tribunal, your first instinct will probably be *heck, yeah!* because supes, right? At least, that would have been *my* first instinct before, you know, I was *forced* to sit in on a supe tribunal because I was subpoenaed (via Dr. Alun Kendrick's broadsword) to testify in a trial that would either condemn the man I loved to possible death or else allow him to marry another guy.

Yeah, good times, that.

This time, the tribunal wasn't quite as uncomfortable. Yes, I had to testify, but only in the fact-finding phase, since I was the lead investigator on the case. Luckily, my testimony cleared the man I—okay, I wasn't willing to say *loved* because one unrequited love affair per lifetime is enough, thank you very much. Let's say the man I found very attractive despite him being a grumpy cuss who was still technically married to one of the most beautiful men I'd ever seen, since said man was still MIA and therefore unavailable for the sundering ceremony that might make said grumpy cuss possibly available.

Whew.

Yeah, so anyway, by the time all the testifying and judgment passing and whatnot was over, both Martinsons—Reid hadn't succeeded in murdering his father *or* Mal, as it turned out, thanks to quick action by the FTA impromptu emergency response squad—were stripped of their rank and possessions, their magic nullified, and consigned to an extremely long stint slinging scrap metal at Govannon's forge, the supe community's version of a maximum security prison, located in the literal underworld, policed by an elder god, and with bonus hard labor.

As for me, I got slapped with a reprimand for breaking into the Martinsons' house. Given the outcome, however, they just extended my probationary period by another six months instead of…whatever else they did with humans who screwed up. We, uh, managed to downplay Jordan's participation and keep him off the tribunal's radar.

Lachlan was cleared of all the charges that the Martinsons had trumped up against him in absentia. He never made it to the tribunal chamber because the Martinsons had staged the *Cridhe na Mara* just outside the bay to support their accusations, and apparently the human Coast Guard had issues with leaving your boat anchored in a shipping channel with nobody aboard. Go figure.

He'd wired Mal the full payment for Quest's work on the case while I was being deposed by a very intimidating sphinx, so I didn't get to say goodbye. Probably for the best, all things considered. Like I said, one unrequited love affair per lifetime is enough.

Zeke had coffee waiting for us when we got back to the offices—me, Mal, Niall, and, surprisingly, Eleri, who'd been instrumental in revealing some of the less savory activities going on in Pierce's workroom.

And no. You *really* don't want to know about those. *I* didn't want to know about those, because there are some images that just don't belong in anybody's mental attic.

Mal and Niall had immediately taken off again, but Eleri settled onto the loveseat against the wall in Mal's office and inhaled the heavenly steam. "Mmmm. Druid-blessed coffee beans."

"How can you tell? Thanks, Zeke," I said, accepting my own mug from him.

She gave me an indignant glare. "I'm a *dryad*."

"As if that explains everything," I muttered.

"Well, it does," Zeke said. "Dryads have an affinity for anything plant based, whether it's still growing or not."

"*Thank* you," Eleri said. "At least somebody around here knows their butt from their elbow."

I scowled at her. "What's that supposed to mean?"

"You could have avoided that extra six months of probation if you'd just *told* me you were looking for Lachlan's pack. You knew I was working against the Martinsons."

I choked on my coffee. "I knew no such thing. When I saw you at their place, you were creating the equivalent of Sleeping Beauty's bramble hedge between Lachlan and Wyn."

She rolled her eyes. "I was blocking *Reid* from *Lachlan*, you ninny. And it wasn't a bramble hedge. I was manifesting a tree of heaven. Which you should have recognized, considering you'd spent hours staring at one."

I narrowed my eyes. "How do you know I was staking out that tree?"

She took a sip of coffee and smirked at me over the cup rim. "I was there, of course."

"So that *was* you! What were you all doing out there anyway?"

The smirk disappeared. She gazed into her cup and mumbled, "It was our book club meeting."

"Book club?" I snorted. "What was this month's selection? *The Wind in the Willows*? *War for the Oaks*? *Fire and Hemlock*?"

She shuddered. "Ugh. Don't mention fire. Especially not at this time of year when everything's so dry."

"Why hide way out there anyway and incur the suspicion of your stick-up-his-ass clan chief?"

She lifted her chin and glared at me. "It's not *really* a book club. That's just our cover. We were meeting to discuss how to move against Martinson. Since the clan chief is so root-bound that he refuses to take any action, we have to sneak around behind his back to get anything done."

"I can understand you all chasing me to begin with—you didn't know who I was and Jordan peed on your tree. But why keep harassing me afterward?"

Her expression turned mischievous. "Because it was fun? Besides, you have to admit it turned out for the best, since we were on site and ready to roll when Reid tried to stage his little coup."

"Yeah. Fortuitous." I wondered if it was a spell, an extra penance the council assessed on me for the crime of being human: that I couldn't meet any supe without an accompanying humiliating event. I stared into my coffee, the urge to fling something—although not a fish—warring with that awful sinking sensation I got in my middle whenever I was reminded I'd *always* be on the outside looking in. "Anyway, the tree of heaven doesn't have thorns," I grumbled.

"I was *accessorizing*." She sniffed. "I was sending you a *message*."

"A pretty dang obscure one."

"A *tree of heaven*." She widened her eyes in a *seriously dude?* expression. "It's an *invasive species*. I was *invading*."

It was my turn to roll my eyes. "Next time, send a text."

"Hey, guys!" Jordan bounced into the room, his arms full of Wonderful Mug bags. "I brought scones!"

I glanced at the coffee tray, which had a full plate of scones right in the middle of it. "Um, why?"

Zeke tilted his head, a perplexed frown pleating his forehead. "You delivered our full order only a couple of hours ago. I didn't make another call. We don't have meetings on the schedule today, not with Mal and Niall tied up in the mage negotiations in Faerie."

Jordan bit his lip. "Weeelll…"

I set my cup down with a sigh. "What is it, Jordan?"

He scuffed one battered trainer against the floor. "The thing is...I, um, may have had another accident with the milk steamer."

"Again?" I checked for bandages, but his hands were clear of gauze. "Did you get it taken care of at St. Stupid's?"

His shoulders hunched and his arms tightened around the bags. Zeke rescued them before the scones could be reduced to crumbs. "I mean, the accident was *to* the milk steamer. I kinda snapped the nozzle off." His eyes widened in an earnest expression. "It'll be okay. I mean, my pack is replacing it. But George, my boss... Well, he's decided maybe Wonderful Mug isn't the best place for me to work." He smiled brightly. "But then I remembered how much I helped you with your cases and I told everybody I could work with Quest!"

I exchanged a glance with Zeke. "Did you run that past Mal or Niall?"

"Well, No. But that won't be a problem, right, once you explain how much I helped you?"

I wouldn't call it "help" exactly. His "help" is what got me in trouble with the dryads, and shielding him from the Martinson break-in had been the major cause of my probation extension. "I'm pretty sure you'll need to talk to them yourself."

"Oh. All right." Cue the sad puppy eyes. "Is it okay if I wait in here with you?" He wrinkled his nose. "Lachlan's in the lobby and you know how I feel about the water."

I sat forward so fast that my coffee sloshed onto my hand. "Lachlan's here? Why?"

Zeke handed me several napkins without a word, and I blotted my hand—and my jeans. "Probably to pick up his pack and his skin."

I paused with a wad of coffee-soaked napkin in my fist. "Didn't he already get it?"

Zeke shook his head. "No. I've got it in the secure supply closet." Another pocket dimension, in case you were wondering, so *super* secure. "He was called away to deal with his boat before the council exonerated him."

"He didn't say anything about the *pack*," Jordan said, his face screwed up so much it had to hurt. "And I would have noticed, because, you know, *pack* is a word I'm *way* too familiar with, but for different reasons."

"Then why is he here?"

Jordan gave me the *seriously dude* look. "To see you, of course."

"M-me? You're sure."

He laughed. "Well, duh. He *said* so."

"Jordan," Zeke said gently, "you didn't actually mention that part."

"Oh." He shrugged. "Sorry?"

I bolted for the door, but Zeke stopped me with a touch on my arm. "Hugh. You should return his skin and property to him."

"*I* should? Why?"

He smiled wryly. "Because you're the human who stole it."

I jerked away. "I didn't *steal* it."

"Well, not from *him*," Jordan mumbled around a mouthful of scone.

I glanced between him, Zeke, and Eleri. "I didn't steal it from anybody. That was Ronnie Purl."

"But Ronnie's a supe," Eleri said as Zeke slipped out of the room. "You're the only human in the equation, the only one who touched it." She shrugged. "Selkies and humans. It's a thing."

"A thing." I couldn't identify the odd sensation in my middle. "What kind of thing?"

She just responded with another smirk. Before I could demand more information, Zeke returned and handed me the pack. "The skin's inside." I took it numbly and stumbled toward the door. "And Hugh?" I glanced over my shoulder at him. "Remember. You're valued. Important. *Special*. What you bring to the table is unique among every human on the planet." He grinned. "Or under it. So don't let him intimidate you or talk you into something you're uncomfortable with."

*Special*, was I? Was that code for clueless and pathetic? "Got it."

I shouldered the pack, those damn rocks—no, *jewels*, for Pete's sake—poking into my back as I took the stairs so fast I almost missed the last step and took a header onto the floor. I caught myself in time, but I was still out of breath when I stumbled into the lobby. Luckily, Lachlan was gazing out the window, so his back was to me, giving me a chance to pull my shirt straight. The coffee-stained jeans were a lost cause.

"Lachlan?"

He spun around, and for a moment, I thought he looked as discombobulated as I did, but that couldn't be right. He was *Lachlan Brodie*. The selkie king, even if he'd refused the throne. Of course, he still looked like Jason Momoa as Aquaman, a look that was really working for me today. "Ah. Matthew. Hello."

I thrust out the pack. "You're probably here for this."

"Thank you." He took it, but set it aside as if it didn't contain the most important thing in his life.

"I've got a question, though." I rubbed my damp palms down the sides of my jeans. "You said you needed the money from those charter bookings."

"Aye. I do."

I pointed at the pack. "Why not sell some of the bling you're humping around in that pack? You've got a king's ransom in gems in there."

He huffed a half laugh. "That's exactly what it is."

"What what is?" I asked, mystified.

"A king's ransom." He met my gaze with what I could swear was sincerity. "They're the selkie crown jewels."

I could fake sincerity with the best of them, so I wasn't buying what he was selling. Not yet. "Shouldn't crown jewels be in a, well, crown?"

He quirked that bisected eyebrow—and apparently I had an eyebrow kink now. "Do I look like the sort of bloke who'd wear a crown?"

I tried to picture it. "Okay. Nope. But in that case—"

"The clans foist them on me, tucking them into some very inconvenient spots on the boat, hoping I'll relent and take the throne. Which, just to be clear, is never happening."

"Then why not just give them back?"

"I've tried!" His exasperation was clear in his tone. "The blighters won't take no for an answer. Every time I send them back, they reappear with another diamond or sapphire or some other useless bauble added on top."

"I suppose," I said slowly, "diamonds beat dead herrings as onboard accessories."

He snorted. "I'd almost prefer the herrings. At least they're good to feed the gulls." His big chest lifted in a sigh. "I'll not take payment for a job I refuse to do, so I'm holding onto the gems in trust, you might say. And since the witches took the protections off my boat, I have to haul them about with me." His expression turned serious. "I'm not rich, Matthew. I'll never be rich."

"Okay? Is this about your Quest bill, because I'm not—"

"That's not... I was rather hoping that you... That we... That is..." He ran his hands through his hair and muttered something under his breath. "I wanted to...thank you. For everything."

"I was just doing my job. Here at Quest, we endeavor to give our clients the best possible service."

Another eyebrow quirk, dammit. "Do you risk your life for all your clients then?"

"I, er..." Was that *interest* in his eyes? "It's never come up before. You were my first case that involved more than surveillance."

"Is that all I was, then?" He took a step closer. "A case?"

Jeez, it was easier to hold my ground against ex-dead Reid Martinson than it was against Lachlan with that glint in his eye. "Y-yes."

"But the case is closed now that I've paid in full." He stopped a good two yards away, thank goodness, and toyed with the stapler on Zeke's desk. "Isn't that right?"

"It's closed, but—" I took a deep breath. "Lachlan, are you hitting on me?"

He winced. "If you can't tell, then I must be more out of practice than I thought."

"It's not that. You're still married. And..." My throat tightened. "Wyn didn't cheat on you on purpose. The Martinsons put a spell on him."

"I know."

I goggled at him. "You do? How?"

"Figured it out on the boat. It doesn't change anything, not for him and not for me. Although...it's complicated."

"Uh huh." I countered with an eyebrow raise of my own. "I've heard that one before."

He uttered a muffled laugh, and his tanned cheeks turned ruddy. "Until Wyn surfaces again, we can't officially sever the knot, so yes, I'm still married, even though our sundering is duly registered and awaiting only our joint audience with the Queen." He moistened his lips with the tip of his tongue. "I won't dishonor my promise. I won't *cheat*. I, ah, don't really trust myself to be alone with you." He glanced at me from under his lashes. "Not for long. But maybe you could come on a sail with Blair and me? The poor mite needs a treat and I want to spend time with you when we're not fighting for our lives. Get to know you better and see whether there might be something between us once I'm free."

Although warmth spread from my belly to my heart and all the way to my fingertips—he was interested in me!—my common sense was ready to douse me in a whole bucket full of ice water. "How long am I supposed to wait?"

His brows came together in confusion. "What?"

"I mean," I said gently, "what if Wyn never comes back?"

His eyes widened, his jaw sagging. Apparently, he'd never considered that. But then his expression cleared and that sly, glint-eyed smile was back. "Well, then, I guess somebody would have to find him." He set the stapler back on the desk and winked at me. "And it so happens I know an excellent private investigator who's just the man for the job."

# WHAT'S NEXT?

◉

CHECK OUT MATT'S NEXT CASE!

# THE HOUND OF THE BURGERVILLES

*This case is really going to the dogs...*

After I try a little off-the-books interrogation to locate my selkie almost-boyfriend's nearly-ex-husband (don't ask, it's complicated), I'm in the doghouse again with my bosses, who bust me back to surveillance. *Ugh.* So when another human inexplicably storms into Quest Investigations—something our security spells ought to prevent since *I'm* supposed to be the only human admitted to our offices—I'm reduced to staking out local fast food restaurants to check out the guy's alleged sighting of a giant, glowing-eyed, dumpster-diving spectral hound.

Ridiculous, right? Humiliating, too, not to mention boring. But at least they didn't fire me.

Imagine my surprise when there actually *is* a giant, glowing-eyed, dumpster-diving spectral hound—one of the Cwn Annwn, Herne the Hunter's traitor-tracking dog pack, to be exact. Jeez, who let *this* dog out? It's my case, though, so it's up to me—Matt Steinitz, aka Hugh Mann—to return him to Faerie. But while Herne's normally hopping kennels are inexplicably unpopulated by pups, they're playing host to one extremely dead body.

Uh oh. Looks like someone's bite was a lot worse than their bark.

Guess my love life will have to take a back seat again while we nose out the truth.

*Dammit.*

# THE HOUND OF THE BURGERVILLES

Eleri squinted at the tor, scanning for something that I couldn't detect. "There."

She took off up the hill with me slogging along behind her. The tor was one of those changeable Faerie geography things— sometimes it could feel like you were scaling Mount Everest and other times it wasn't any more strenuous than hiking over the Nike campus berm. Today it was somewhere in the middle, so by the time we got to the top and stopped inside a dense grove of alder and birch, I was breathing heavily but not about to pass out. Eleri, of course, looked as fresh as she had in the line at Wonderful Mug, although considerably more awake.

"Grizel's stream is through there." She pointed at what appeared to be a solid wall of tree trunks.

"How the heck are we supposed to get the lay of the land? I may be a surveillance specialist, but I can't see through *that*."

She shrugged. "So move the trees."

It was my turn to give her the *Seriously?* glare. "Now is not the time for dryad humor, Eleri."

"For a change, I'm not joking."

"Fine. I'll bite. How the heck to I get trees to move?"

"Ask them nicely." For an instant, she maintained her poker face, but then she relented and grinned at me. "Chill, BFF. I've got you." She strode forward and placed one palm on a birch, the other on a neighboring alder, murmuring something I couldn't hear clearly but which sounded like Welsh.

And the trees moved aside.

"Damn. You're good," I said.

Eleri just winked at me and gestured for me to follow her. We crept through the magically less dense copse until we could peer out through the underbrush to the hillside beyond.

Grizel was there, all right, in all her blue-skinned glory. She wasn't tall—probably a handspan shorter than Eleri who barely topped five feet—although her knot of iron gray hair, held in place by some kind of bone, added another inch or three. She was wearing the same ankle-length green skirt and faded, loose-knit shawl that she'd been wearing the first time I'd seen her, so either she only had one set of clothes or she had a really consistent fashion sense.

On the other hand, if you were called the Washerwoman of Death, who knew how you handled your own laundry?

Several garments already hung from low-hanging branches of the gnarled oak tree about halfway down the slope. She had a couple of clothespins gripped between her teeth as she lifted a limp shirt out of the wicker basket at her feet.

"Uh oh," Eleri murmured. "Somebody's number is up."

"Let me do the talking, okay? She can be really literal about what constitutes a question, and we can only ask three." I'd been formulating them for the last week, turning them over in my mind to make sure they couldn't be interpreted more than one way, and I was convinced I had them nailed. Wyn was as good as found already, and then Lachlan and I could get on with…getting it on. "Just block her access to the stream as fast as you can because if she makes it into the water, she doesn't have to answer." And once we tipped our hand, our chances of successfully ambushing her again would be precisely zero.

"I'm not an idiot," Eleri hissed. "I know how this works."

"Okay. You head for the stream and I'll herd her toward you. But she's quicker than she looks, so don't dawdle."

"Don't worry," she said, lowering into a sprinter's crouch. "If I can outrun a forest fire, I can outrun her."

"Ready. Set. Go!"

We launched ourselves out of the trees, Eleri speeding toward the stream bank while I angled toward Grizel. She saw me—I know she saw me, because she stared right at me—but she didn't do anything other than spit out the clothespins and bare an alarming array of pointed yellow teeth.

*Uh oh.* I remembered something from our first encounter—she'd believed I'd been some kind of tribute, a gift to her from Mal, in exchange for information.

Maybe tackling her without his backup wasn't my most brilliant notion.

I started to slow my pace, but before I could veer off to the side, something streaked past me, clipping my hip and sending me staggering into the laundry.

While I was wrestling with a face full of wet suede—*ewww*—Grizel shouted a curse in Gaelic. When I finally pulled the clinging fabric off my head, she was charging down the hillside, a lean wolf with a telltale white blaze on his flank nipping at her heels.

"Jordan," I groaned. "Of course it had to be Jordan."

The young werewolf had started interning at Quest at the same time Eleri hired on, and he was nothing if not enthusiastic. Unfortunately, he didn't possess a lot of common sense and if he'd ever considered the consequences of his actions before he plowed full steam ahead, I'd never heard about it.

Eleri was crouching at the stream's edge, her arms spread, her fingers sprouting leaves and her signature thorn accessories, a resolute expression on her face. While Grizel hadn't run from me, Jordan, as reckless as he was, was getting the job done of driving her toward Eleri. Okay, this might work out after all.

But then Grizel reached into the pocket of her apron, and her arm flew in a windup any major league pitcher would envy.

"Fetch!" she called.

Jordan's gaze immediately snapped to follow the trajectory of whatever she'd sent sailing through the air and he took off after it, crashing through the underbrush in his eagerness.

Grizel cackled, then calmly strolled the last few yards toward the stream, neatly bypassing Eleri who, for some reason, didn't try to stop her. Grizel stepped into the water on extremely large bare blue feet, then turned to smirk at us.

"Safe," she said. "Tha great ninnies."

Dear Reader,

Thank you so much for reading *Five Dead Herrings*, the inaugural book in my Quest Investigations mystery series! If you're curious about Matt's backstory, you might want to check out his debut on the Mythmatched stage in *Single White Incubus*, the first in the Supernatural Selection trilogy about a paranormal matchmaking agency. If you'd like to go all the way back to the Mythmatched beginnings, the story world dawned with *Cutie and the Beast*, a paranormal rom-com where a cursed fae warrior turned psychologist clashes with his determined temporary office manager. As you might expect, hijinks ensue!

You can see all my books on my website, https://ejrussell.com, or on my Amazon author page here: https://www.amazon.com/author/cj_russell. Most are also available at Apple, Kobo, and Barnes and Noble.

Would you like exclusive content and ARC giveaways, not to mention gratuitous dance videos? Then I'd love for you to join me in Reality Optional, my Facebook fan group (https://facebook.com/groups/reality.optional). My newsletter is the place to get the latest dish on new releases, sales, and more. I promise I only send one out when I've got…well…news. You can subscribe here: https://ejrussell.com/newsletter.

All my best,
—E

ALSO BY
# E.J. RUSSELL

**Paranormal Romance**
*Mythmatched Universe*
*Fae Out of Water Trilogy*
Cutie and the Beast
The Druid Next Door
Bad Boy's Bard

*Supernatural Selection Trilogy*
Single White Incubus
Vampire With Benefits
Demon on the Down-Low

*Other Mythmatched Romances*
Howling on Hold
Possession in Session
Witch Under Wraps
Cursed is the Worst
The Skinny on Djinni

*Mythmatched Companion Stories*
Rusty's Really Bad Day (free to newsletter subscribers)
Second First Date (free to newsletter subscribers)

*Quest Investigations Mysteries*
Five Dead Herrings
The Hound of the Burgervilles
The Lady Under the Lake

Death on Denial

*Art Medium Series*
The Artist's Touch
Tested in Fire
Art Medium: The Complete Collection (omnibus edition)

*Legend Tripping Series*
Stumptown Spirits
Wolf's Clothing

*Enchanted Occasions Series*
Best Beast
Nudging Fate
Devouring Flame

*Royal Powers Series* (shared world)
Duking It Out
Duke the Hall
King's Ex

*Magic Emporium Series* (shared world)
Purgatory Playhouse

Monster Till Midnight

**Historical Romance**
Silent Sin

**Contemporary Romance**
Camera Shy
The Thomas Flair
Mystic Man
For a Good Time, Call… (A Bluewater Bay novel, with Anne Tenino)

## ABOUT THE
# AUTHOR

E.J. Russell (she/her), author of the award-winning Mythmatched paranormal romance series, writes LGBTQ+ romance and mystery in a rainbow of flavors. Count on high snark, low angst, and happy endings.

Reality? Eh, not so much.

She's married to Curmudgeonly Husband, a man who cares even less about sports than she does. Luckily, C.H. also loves to cook, or all three of their children (Lovely Daughter and Darling Sons A and B) would have survived on nothing but Cheerios, beef jerky, and Satsuma mandarins (the extent of E.J.'s culinary skill set).

E.J. also writes traditional cozy mystery as Nelle Heran. She lives in rural Oregon, enjoys visits from her wonderful adult children, and indulges in good books, red wine, and the occasional hyperbole.

*News & Social Media:*
Website: https://ejrussell.com
Newsletter: https://ejrussell.com/newsletter

# ACKNOWLEDGEMENTS

Many thanks to my awesome beta readers—Kelly Jensen, Meghan Maslow, and lyric apted—for suggestions, advice, and encouragement; to Meg DesCamp for editing magic; to L.C. Chase for the adorable cover; to my family for endless support; and of course to you, my readers, for accompanying me on this wild journey.

Without all of you, I wouldn't be able to continue to do what I love.